"This is a dynamic work, a re-crea
than a recollection of it in tranq·
ness and imaginative power are such as to involve the reader in ......
may have begun as an act of personal liberation."
—MICHAEL HAMBURGER,
THE TIMES LITERARY SUPPLEMENT

"[Weiss's *Aesthetics of Resistance*] is a magnum opus which sees itself,
almost programmatically, not only as the expression of an ephemeral
wish for redemption, but as an expression of the *will* to be on the side
of the victims at the end of time."   —W. G. SEBALD,
FROM *ON THE NATURAL HISTORY OF DESTRUCTION*

"Bertolt Brecht comes automatically to mind, but Weiss's style has its
own hypnotic force."   —*THE NEW YORK TIMES*

"Peter Weiss is one of the most interesting dramatists writing now . . .
To accept his work plain is to miss the whole point; he seems to want
to put on stage huge explosions of the instinctual life, instincts that
have become politicized, but are not merely politics."
—ELIZABETH HARDWICK,
THE NEW YORK REVIEW OF BOOKS

"A great novel . . . Weiss's account takes us through familiar territory
by new routes, so that we see the landmarks as we have never seen
them before."   —*THE HUDSON REVIEW*

"Must be counted among the most important European authors of the
20th century."   —*THE COMPLETE REVIEW*

"Yes, *The Aesthetics of Resistance* is intimidating. But it is also ex-
hilaratingly strange, compelling, and original. Readers who dare
enter this demanding verbal landscape will not come away empty-
handed."   —*BOOKFORUM*

LEAVETAKING

PETER WEISS (1916–1982) was born in the Prussian province of Brandenburg to a Jewish father, who had converted to Lutheranism, and a Christian mother. He spent his childhood in Bremen and, as an adolescent, began his studies in the visual arts in Berlin. In the early thirties, with the rise of the Nazi Party in Germany, the family immigrated first to England and then Sweden. Weiss studied photography and painting at the Polytechnic School of Photography and the Prague Art Academy. He began to correspond with Hermann Hesse, who became a friend and mentor. In 1939, Weiss followed his family to Stockholm, where he would spend the rest of his life, receiving Swedish citizenship in 1946. His first play, *The Tower*, was produced in 1950, and he joined the Swedish Experimental Film Studio soon after. But his greatest international success was in the theater: in 1965, the director Peter Brook staged his play *The Persecution and Assassination of Jean-Paul Marat as Performed by the Inmates of the Asylum of Charenton Under the Direction of the Marquis de Sade* in London and New York, winning multiple Tony Awards. Weiss's politically engaged drama also included *The Investigation*, about the Frankfurt Auschwitz Trial. A multitalented artist, Weiss wrote fiction throughout his career, and he spent the last decade of his life working on a monumental three-part historical novel, *The Aesthetics of Resistance*, which W. G. Sebald referred to in *On the Natural History of Destruction* as a "magnum opus." Weiss died at the age of sixty-five in Stockholm.

CHRISTOPHER LEVENSON is an acclaimed Canadian poet and translator. He is a cofounder of *Arc Poetry Magazine* and the Harbinger Poetry imprint of Carleton University Press.

SVEN BIRKERTS is a literary critic and essayist. His many books include *The Gutenberg Elegies* and *The Other Walk*.

THE NEVERSINK LIBRARY

I was by no means the only reader of books on board the Neversink. Several other sailors were diligent readers, though their studies did not lie in the way of belles-lettres. Their favourite authors were such as you may find at the book-stalls around Fulton Market; they were slightly physiological in their nature. My book experiences on board of the frigate proved an example of a fact which every book-lover must have experienced before me, namely, that though public libraries have an imposing air, and doubtless contain invaluable volumes, yet, somehow, the books that prove most agreeable, grateful, and companionable, are those we pick up by chance here and there; those which seem put into our hands by Providence; those which pretend to little, but abound in much. —HERMAN MELVILLE, *WHITE JACKET*

LEAVETAKING

PETER WEISS

TRANSLATED BY CHRISTOPHER LEVENSON
INTRODUCTION BY SVEN BIRKERTS

MELVILLE HOUSE PUBLISHING
BROOKLYN · LONDON

LEAVETAKING

Originally published under the title *Abschied von den Eltern*

Copyright © 1961 by Suhrkamp Verlag, Frankfurt am Main
Translation copyright © 1967 by Calder Publications
Published by arrangement with Alma Classics Ltd.
Introduction copyright © 2014 by Sven Birkerts

First Melville House printing: July 2014

Melville House Publishing   8 Blackstock Mews
   145 Plymouth Street   and   Islington
   Brooklyn, NY 11201   London N4 2BT

mhpbooks.com   facebook.com/mhpbooks   @melvillehouse

Library of Congress Cataloging-in-Publication Data

Weiss, Peter, 1916–1982.
  [*Abschied von den Eltern*. English]
  Leavetaking / Peter Weiss ; Translated by Christopher
  Levenson ; Introduction by Sven Birkerts.
    pages   cm
  ISBN 978-1-61219-331-1 (pbk.)
  ISBN 978-1-61219-332-8 (ebook)
  I. Levenson, Christopher, 1934– translator.   II. Title.

PT2685.E5A6213 2014
833'.914—dc23

               2013045408

Design by Christopher King

Printed in the United States of America
1 3 5 7 9 10 8 6 4 2

INTRODUCTION
BY SVEN BIRKERTS

The German-born novelist, dramatist, artist, and film-maker Peter Weiss, who adopted Swedish national-ity after World War II, is part of that generation of German-speaking writers (including Heinrich Böll, Al-fred Andersch, and Max Frisch) who came into young manhood in the years preceding the war and whose work almost inevitably explores questions of power and morality within that historical frame. In the decade leading up to his death, Weiss—who is best known for his play *Marat/Sade*—was finishing what many consider to be his masterwork, the three-volume *The Aesthetics of Resistance*, of which only the first volume has been translated into English. That novel, as its title suggests, takes on the vast subject of the European opposition to the rise of Nazism. Another play of Weiss's, *The Investi-gation*, meanwhile, assembles documentary evidence to assess the findings of the Frankfurt Auschwitz Trial. His claim on posterity would seem to be as a key figure of witness and moral inquiry.

Readers may well be surprised to discover, there-fore, that the writer had a powerful and highly refined subjective register as well, displayed in his surrealism-inspired paintings (he'd studied first to be a painter) as well as in a pair of imagistically compressed auto-biographical novellas, *Leavetaking* (1961) and *Vanishing Point* (1962). Indeed, so intense is Weiss's sentence-by-sentence charge in this mode that one could be excused for assuming it is his central expressive register.

Coming-of-age is, of course, one of the great archetypes. And the basic narrative template is familiar. The narrator/protagonist is depicted as alienated from the outside world as well as from family; there are bitter struggles over the failure to conform. Great ambitions and great loves are nurtured in an uncomprehended privacy. Until eventually comes the breakaway. He (in this version of archetype, it is usually a young man) experiences the travails of formation—conflicts, losses, and sunderings—but at last finds himself standing, if teetering a bit, on his own two feet.

There is nothing new in Weiss's use of this narrative pattern in *Leavetaking*. The stages are ones we recognize, yet through every page this short work is arresting, confirming—if confirmation were needed—that much important art is a matter of the *how* rather than the *what*. Which is not to discount the subject matter, only to stress how often it is the treatment that shows the hand of the master.

Leavetaking projects a distinctive tone, a decisive confidence, and captures with complete freshness a sensibility in development. This confidence is manifest immediately in Weiss's declarative opening:

> I have often tried to come to an understanding of the images of my father and my mother, to take bearings and steer a course between rebellion and submission. But I have never been able to grasp and interpret the essential being of these two figures standing at either side of the gateway of my life. Both died almost at the same time and it was then I saw how deeply estranged I was from them.

Though Weiss begins with an admission of uncertainty, he does so with a frankness that will be carried through in every line of this unscrolling account of his younger years. I use the adjective "unscrolling" deliberately, for the author appears to be an early pioneer of the unparagraphed text, and the visually effortful—at times frustrating—business of reading this novel-as-memoir from start to finish is clearly part of its intent. But what is such a choice of presentation stating? That life will pause for no organizing afterthought; that in the chaos of becoming, immediacy is the rule; that it is better to preserve this sense of an undifferentiated onrush than to try to wrest from events an impression of circumstance mastered in retrospect?

Weiss achieves these effects, and after a few pages during which we experience that "irritable reaching after fact and reason" that Keats described in one of his letters, there is (there was for me) a shift to acceptance. While it is not exactly a stream of consciousness that the author is deploying, it is definitely a refusal of easy narrative footholds. Weiss wants us to take away a sense of relentlessness, of exacerbated awareness, the sensations of a life that has thus far (it ends in the narrator's young manhood) attained no vantage of comprehension.

This suspension of narrative norms extends deep into the structure of Weiss's account, for though the events that take him from his earliest days to the emancipation augured in the title are narrated in essential sequence, they in no way correspond to expected proportions. Particular childhood moments distend into pockets of duration, requiring our close regard of the least granular detail. Events and transitions that would seem to demand extended exposition are sometimes accomplished within the space of a sentence, and as the sentences come to us in undifferentiated flow, the imagined import is radically reframed. Changes of country, whole years of immersed activity—as they used to say of those small highway-side towns (before the advent of the commercial strip), "If you blink, you'll miss it." What we experience is the absolutism of memory, memory given full editorial control, a project not unlike the one pursued by Virginia Woolf in her densely lyrical—and sometimes maddeningly intermittent—essays, like "A Sense of the Past." The work is doing double duty, offering at once an exposure to the sensations and events of the life *and* a portrait of the mechanism of recollection itself. Welding the two together is a feeling, understood explicitly at the very end, that the whole presentation reveals the psychological stages of the narrator's core formation, what he understands as his destiny as an artist and as a man.

The original ambush of recollection, which leads us back into the first stirrings of this formation, happens in the narrator's parents' house, where he and his siblings have gathered after the death of his father—the second of his parents to die—in order to bury him and divide up his possessions. The grim, affectless scene reveals straightaway that all members of the family are estranged and that emotional alienation is the banner under which they move. Weiss stands in the echoing space, looking out through the tinted panes of the glass door to the garden. He reflects:

> At the time of this viewing, my basic nature had already been formed, and only when the observing, controlling part of me wearies and my consciousness loses its hold do impulses arise in me out of my earliest life, and it is in half sleep, in dreams, in periods of depression that I re-experience the helplessness, the feeling of having been handed over and the blind rebellion of the time when strange hands tamed, kneaded, and did violence to my being.

The key signature has now been established. From here on the author carries us along through a subjective impressionism that is at once fluid in its feeling, rolling on and on through the long, unparagraphed sentences that are strikingly—vividly—particular in their detailing. As when he captures his early sense of his street, which "in the green twilight was full of the trundling of drays laden high with barrels," and where the "heavy, sweet smell swelled in waves from the breweries."

Such a crowd of sensory recollections! Alongside these, gradually emerging like a photograph in a developing tray, is a portrait of the family: the distant mother; the overworked and submissive father; the siblings; and the strong counterbalancing presence of Augusta, cook and housekeeper. It is Augusta who takes the boy out on what is for him an epic exploration of the city; in her presence is the world made vivid and tactile, a complete contrast to his sense of the cold, quiet rooms at home.

In these opening pages, too, the narrator meets the neighbor boy, Friederle, a sadistic tormentor—every young life has one—who we will later learn, very obliquely, became an enthusiastic partisan of the Reich. The obliquity of the revelation matters here, for it is very much Weiss's intent—even though his coming-of-age is contemporaneous with the rise of National Socialism and, later, the war—to have the focus reflect emphatically a young man's nonpolitical self-absorption. We deduce the historical situation, and here and there get flashes of the temper of the times, but the intensities represented are nearly all interior and private. There is no question, though, that the unstated historical is present throughout—it saturates the pages with atmospheric dread; we feel it everywhere in the wings.

As the narrative progresses, Weiss plaits together various thematic strands. These can be itemized—named—but doing so suggests that they are separable, when in fact they are not. Sexuality, struggles for autonomy within the family, the rearing up of a powerful expressive impulse—these and other forces are densely entangled here. Uncensored eruptions of adolescent lust veer toward the incestuous. Their repressed intensity underscores the guilt, rage, and isolation that have everything to do with the relations between father and son, and, too, with the boy's need to paint images and, later, to begin writing.

To try to elicit a clear narrative or thematic sequence from a work that has evolved its uniquely expressive form precisely to convey the dense subjective interpenetration of event and implication seems a violation. Indeed, the point, manifest in the prose throughout, is that the business of formations, as experienced and as then later refracted through memory, is profoundly alchemical. We need only take tissue samples of the prose, and these can be taken anywhere.

Midway through the work, for instance, with a characteristic abruptness, we learn of his sister Margit's mysterious, traumatic death. The event is unexpected, unprepared-for; it rears up with a frightening hallucinatory force. Weiss characterizes it as "the beginning of the break-up of our family," intensifying all sorrow, heightening the already painful distances between the narrator and his parents, neither of whom have any way to integrate the loss. Here, as elsewhere, the movement of the prose showcases Weiss's way of bending together exposition, confessionalism, and the wounding vibrancy of select details. He describes his own state of mind after Margit's death:

Past events rose up in me like a gasping for breath, like the pressure of a straitjacket, the past would hem me around in a slow, black seepage of hours, and then suddenly recede and become nothing and allow a brief glimpse of freedom. Then I saw my parents and was full of sympathy and compassion. They had given us all that they had to give, they had given us food and clothing and a civilized home, they had given us their security and their orderliness and they could not understand why we did not thank them for it. They could never understand why we drifted away from them ... Thus we confronted each other, children dissatisfied, parents insulted ... My parents' embarrassment became my embarrassment. Their voices live on in me. I chastised and beat myself and drove myself to forced labor. Again and again the swamp fever of inadequacy gripped me. There I was again, a failure at school, sitting locked into my room, and the warm seething life outside was unattainable. There sat my mother next to me and heard me repeat my lessons and I could get nothing right. Schwein is pig, pig comes from to pick—pick, pick, pick, and she took hold of me by the scruff of the neck and pressed my nose into the vocabulary book, pick, pick, pick, so now perhaps you'll remember it.

We note the piling on of urgent analogies, the rhetorical repetitions of exposition ("they had given us ..."), and then the insistent and tactile immediacy of the mother's coercions. The pressure builds as Weiss creates the picture, the inward accounting, of how it was, from earliest childhood constraints on through the long years of psychological entrapment, during which he worked in a reluctant servitude as his father's assistant, all the while building what rocket engineers call the "exit velocity."

However, even attaining that is a fraught and long-term process. It requires that the young man get away, leave the country—there is a Hesse-like "master" he seeks out—but then, following a Beckettian script of enmeshment, he becomes entrapped again. He returns home and finds himself thrust back down into what feels like a timeless well of failure. It's as if the terms of life are set in stone. But then at long last, and seemingly not because of anything he has done or prepared, but rather because something long in the maturing is finally ready, he does break free: he achieves his eponymous leavetaking. And this, when it comes—because of the prose—does not feel like a resolution from without, but very much an attainment from within, a moment destined from the start, its arrival encoded in his processing of every last twist and turn in his experience.

Interestingly, the time span of *Leavetaking* is an overview very similar to that of Joyce's *A Portrait of the Artist as a Young Man*. It, too, launches from the sometimes dreamlike distensions and distortions of a young boy's hyper-intense subjectivity, and ends in his assertive young manhood. Both books also end in what feels like a headlong rush of momentum: Joyce's

Stephen Daedalus pitches forth with grandiose fanfare, fleeing the captivity of home to "forge the yet uncreated conscience of his race." Weiss's unparagraphed prose, meanwhile, compels a reader's involvement, but also the breath-held sense of anticipated release. When that re-lease—the white space—comes, it correlates utterly with the narrator's final announcement: "I was on my way to look for a life of my own."

LEAVETAKING

I HAVE OFTEN TRIED TO COME TO AN understanding of the images of my father and my mother, to take bearings and steer a course between rebellion and submission. But I have never been able to grasp and interpret the essential being of these two figures standing at either side of the gateway of my life. Both died almost at the same time and it was then I saw how deeply estranged I was from them. The grief that overcame me was not for them, for I hardly knew them, the grief was for what had been missed, for the yawning emptiness that surrounded my childhood and youth. Grief sprang from the recognition that the attempt at togetherness in which the members of the family had persisted to the end for two whole decades had completely failed. My sorrow was for the sense of too-lateness that lay on us, brothers and sister, at the graveside, that afterward again drove us apart, each off into his own existence. After my mother's death, my father, whose whole life had been given over to working tirelessly, once again tried to evoke the appearance of a fresh start. He set out on a trip to Belgium, to establish business connections there, as he said, but really to die like a wounded animal in its lair. He went as a broken man, able to move only with difficulty, helped by two canes. When, after learning in Ghent of his death, I had landed at the Brussels airport, with heavy heart I retraced the long trek my father must have had to make, upstairs, downstairs, through hall and corridors on legs enfeebled by poor circulation. It was early March, clear sky, sharp sunlight, a cold wind over Ghent. I went along the street by the railroad embankment, on to the hospital and its chapel where my father had been laid out. Freight cars were being shunted on the tracks behind bare, lopped trees. The cars were rolling and clanking up on the embankment as I stood before the chapel, which looked like a garage, and whose double-door a nun opened for me. Inside, next to a coffin covered with flowers and wreaths, lay my father on a cloth-draped bier, dressed in a black suit now too large for him, in black socks, and with his arms folded across his chest, embracing the framed photograph of my mother. His gaunt face was relaxed, the thin hair, hardly gray at all, curling in one soft lock over his brow, and something of pride, boldness I had never noticed in him before stamped on his features. His hands were perfect, the fingernails symmetrical, bluishly shimmering mussel shells. I stroked the cold, yellowish, taut skin of his hands, while the Sister waited out in the sun a few steps behind me. I recalled my father as I had last seen him, lying on the living-room sofa under a blanket after my mother's burial, his face gray and blurry, blotted out by tears, his mouth stammering and whispering the name of the deceased. I stood there frozen, felt the cold wind, heard the whistles and puffs of steam coming from the

railroad embankment, and there before me a life become a completely closed account, an enormous outlay
of energy dissolved into nothingness. Before me lay the
corpse of a man in an alien land, no longer reachable, a
corpse in a shed by the railroad embankment, a man in
whose life there had been office spaces and hotel rooms,
and always large dwellings, big houses with many rooms
filled with furniture, and in this man's life there had always been the wife who waited for him in the house
they shared, and there had been children in this man's
life, children whom he always shied away from and with
whom he could never talk, but when he was away from
the house he could perhaps feel tenderness for his children and longing for them, and always he carried pictures of them with him and certainly looked at them, all
worn out, creased from so much handling, nights in hotel rooms when he was away on his trips, certainly believing that this time on his return he would find trust,
but when he got back there was always disappointment
and the impossibility of mutual understanding. In this
man's life there had been ceaseless effort to support
home and family, amid worries and sickness, together
with his wife, and he had stuck fast to owning his own
home, without ever experiencing happiness in it. This
man, who now lay lost before me, had never given up
believing in the ideal of a permanent home, but he had
suffered death far away from this home alone in a sickroom, and if at his last breath he had stretched out his
hand to the bell, it would have been, perhaps, to call for
something, for some kind of help, some kind of relief, in

the face of suddenly rising coldness and emptiness. I looked into my father's face, I still alive and preserving within me the knowledge of my father's existence, into a face in shadow grown strange to me. With an expression of contentment he lay in his remoteness, and somewhere his last large house was still standing, piled high with carpets, furniture, potted plants, and pictures, a home that could no longer breathe, a home that he had kept intact throughout the years of emigration, through the constant resettlements and difficulties in adapting to new environments and through the war. Later that day my father was laid in a plain brown coffin that I had bought at the undertaker's and the nun took care that the picture of his wife stayed in his arms, and after the lid had been screwed tight two hospital porters to the accompaniment of continuous rumbling and clattering of freight trains carried the coffin to the hearse, which I followed in a hired car. Here and there at the side of the road to Brussels, farm laborers and workmen, lit up by the afternoon sun, took off their caps to the black car in which my father, for the last time, journeyed through a foreign country. The cemetery with the crematorium lay on a rise outside the city, and the gravestones and bare trees were besieged by a cold wind. In the circular chapel the coffin was placed on a pedestal, I stood next to it and waited, and at a harmonium in an alcove sat an elderly man with the face of a drinker playing a psalm tune, and then in the middle section of the wall a sliding door suddenly opened, and imperceptibly the pedestal with the coffin set itself in motion and slid slowly on almost invisible rails sunk in the floor into the bare, rectangular chamber behind the door, which noiselessly shut again. Two hours later I collected the urn with the ashes of my father's body. I carried the urn container, which had a crown on it and widened out at top, amid looks of consternation past hotel staff and guests up to my room, where I placed it first on the table, then on the windowsill, then on the floor, then on the dressing table, and finally in the wardrobe. I went down into town to buy paper and string in a department store, then wrapped the box in it and spent the night in the hotel with the remains of my father hidden in the wardrobe. Next day I reached my parents' house, where my step-brothers and their wives, my brother and his wife, my sister and her husband awaited me for the burial, the reading of the will, and the apportioning of property. In the days that followed, the final disintegration of the family was completed. A desecration and crushing underfoot took place, full of the undertones of envy and avarice, although outwardly we tried to preserve a friendly and considerate tone of cordial agreement. Even for us, although we had long since become alienated from them, all the articles collected there had their value, and suddenly a wealth of recollections attached itself to each item. The grandfather clock with the sun face had ticked its way into my earliest dreams, in the mirror of the huge wardrobe I had caught sight of myself in the moonlight during my nocturnal excursions, in the diagonal supports beneath the dining-room table I had built dens and dugouts, and had crept behind the rotting velvet curtains to escape the savage pine marten, and many of the books on the high, wide bookshelves contained secret, forbidden things to read. We pushed and shoved around the chairs, sofas, and tables, violently we disrupted the order that had always been unassailable, and soon the house resembled a furniture warehouse and the objects that had been afforded a lifetime's care and protection at my mother's hand lay piled up in various rooms in five huge heaps, some to be taken away, some to be sold. The carpets were rolled up, the pictures lifted down from the walls, the curtains torn from the windows, the cupboards ransacked of crockery and clothes, and the women ran up and down between the attic and the cellar, seizing here an apron, there a wooden spoon, here a box with worn-out dusty shoes, there a coal bucket or a rake. The urns of Father and Mother stood side by side in wet, black cemetery earth, and we brothers and sisters crouched among the fragments of a dismembered home, we drained the bottles from my father's wine cellar and broke open his bureau to sort out his correspondence and documents. In accordance with his last will, mountains of paper were piled up to be burned. Secretly I took some yellowed pages in my father's hand and a few diaries with notes by my mother. The naked bulbs shone harshly in all the rooms and were reflected in the black windowpanes. I had a feeling that the door opened, that my mother had appeared, to stare open-mouthed at her children's ghostly activity. Something died in each of us during these days. Now, after the plundering, we saw that this

home from which we had been thrust out had nevertheless embodied a security for us, and that with its going
the last symbol of our unity disappeared. At the deepest
level of the changes this house had gone through lay
rooms, spaces in which I had emerged from mythic
darkness into first consciousness. I stood in the first-
floor vestibule looking first through one of the red, then
through one of the blue panes of the glass door into the
garden, so making the bushes, the pear tree, the gravel
path, the lawn, and the summer house appear first in a
fiery glow and then in subdued, submarine tones. At the
time of this viewing, my basic nature had already been
formed, and only when the observing, controlling part
of me wearies and my consciousness loses its hold do
impulses arise in me out of my earliest life, and it is in
half sleep, in dreams, in periods of depression that I re-
experience the helplessness, the feeling of having been
handed over and the blind rebellion of the time when
strange hands tamed, kneaded, and did violence to my
being. When my mother once told me the first words I
ever said were What a nice life I have, what a nice life, in
it I heard the ring of something that had been drummed
into my head, parrot-taught, something with which I
had wanted to amuse or mock those around me. Like an
evil spirit I came into this house, lying in a tin box carried by my mother, received by wild tom-tom beats and
my stepbrothers' exorcismal cries. My mother had
found me at the edge of a pond among the rushes and
storks. The first house has large blind spots in it. I can't
find my way through this house, can only dimly

remember the steps of a staircase, the corner of a floor
on which I built little red-brown houses with blocks
grown greasy from so much handling and green re-
doubts, dimly recall a little toy truck filled with miniature boxes, and the thought of those boxes brings back a
thick, heavy sensation in the roof of my mouth. I vaguely
recall postage stamps spread out before me, rose-colored
and light green stamps with the face of a king with
twirled mustaches and my older brothers rushing in and
shouting, and my mother sweeping the stamps together
and throwing them into the stove. And there is the edge
of a tiled stove and the arms of a sofa and I sit on one
arm of the sofa and one of my brothers tickles me and I
fall backward onto the edge of the stove and knock a
hole into my head and some liquid is poured out of a
bottle into the hole in my head and my head froths and
all the sense runs out of my head. I see a room that is
green, the floor green, the curtains green, the wallpaper
green, and I am sitting on a raised porcelain vessel
shaped like a guitar and my mother stands in back of me
and shoves her forefinger into my bum just above the
anus, and I push and she pushes and everything is green,
and the street outside is green, and the street is called
Green Street, the street in the green twilight was full of
the trundling of drays laden high with barrels. The hoofs
of the heavy shaggy horses struck sparks from the cob-
blestones, the coachmen clicked their tongues and
cracked their whips and a heavy, sweet smell swelled in
waves from the breweries. Our house, with its high ga-
bles on whose ridge I rode a race against the moon and

from whose chimney I sprang with a leap into the sky,
lay narrow and squashed between warehouses and the
wall of a factory yard. Once a man climbed over our
roof, there was commotion in the streets and shots rang
out, and my brothers stormed through the house and
shouted that someone had fled onto our roof and men
rushed in from the street into our house, and the men
carried guns in their hands, and they all ran into the
garden and switched on their flashlights and shot up at
the roof and the wounded man fell from the roof down
to the men in the garden below. The house remains
strange to me, I cannot find my way around its interior,
but I take the garden for my own, I lie stretched out on
the ground under the bushes, feel the dry earth between
my hands, put the earth into my mouth, crunch the
earth between my teeth, feel the white, round pebbles,
put the pebbles in my mouth, feel on my tongue their
roundness and the warmth of the sun. Closeness, a shut-
in feeling reigned in the house, and my senses were
trapped. Here out of doors my senses could expand and
when I entered the summer house I entered a kingdom
that belonged only to me, my self-chosen place of exile.
In the narrow bands of sunlight that slanted down
through a high, ivy-mantled window, I steered my vehicle, a little handcart with its upright shaft, between
stacked garden chairs, baskets, and tools, I drove with it,
swam with it, flew with it, humming and murmuring to
myself. This is like a picture from an old book of fairy
tales; something sunken wells up out of the picture,
something fraught with expectancy. The secluded and

the secretive, the hiding away with myself and my games, this is still with me and stirs at this very hour, it is to be felt every time I get lost in my work. I was my own master, I created the world for myself. But somewhere lurked the foresense of a calling out for me, of a call about to ring out, which would come rolling toward me across the garden. The anticipation of this summons was always lurking somewhere, to this very day the anticipation persists, to this day the fear that all can end suddenly. When it called for me the first time, I pretended to be deaf, I kept the calling at arms' length, through being alone I had forgotten my name, I behaved as if it was not meant for me. But then the name was hurled into me again and again until it filled me completely, until I almost burst with it, and I had to answer, I had to confess that the name had found me. I often tried to call myself something else, but when the calling of my only true name whirred toward me, I started, it stuck into me like a harpoon, and I could not avoid it. In a whisper I call to myself with my own name, and frighten myself with it, as if the name came up to me from far outside me from a time in which I was still without form. And then I feel a raving, impotent rage, a storming against the impregnable, and then my stammering is stifled by an invisible hand. There is my mother's face. I flew upward to this face, lifted by her arms, which could enfold all spaces. The face took me up and thrust me from itself. The large, warm mass of the face, with its dark eyes, suddenly became a wolfish grimace with menacing teeth. Out of the hot, white breasts, where drippy milk glands had been a moment before, darted the licking tongues of little snakeheads. Hands had been there earlier than the face. They grabbed me, ripped me up into the air, shook me, sprang at my ears and into my hair. Everything roared and surged about my mother's form. I tried to escape her power by closing my eyes and pressing my lips together over my voice. But then I could no longer endure it, and had to open my eyes wide to cry for my mother's face, and have it proved to me that it was still there. Around my mother everything was unstable, seething, swirling. But next to her stood Augusta, clearly outlined, mild and permanent. From the very first, Augusta was old, old as time. In her black, tightly laced dress, her hands softened by dishwater, red and swollen, Augusta stood clearly outlined in space, and everything that came near her increased its radiance. In my mother reigned the wild and unbridled, in Augusta sufferance, humility. When my mother shouted at her, Augusta bent deep over the white potato basin with the blue rim and the potato peelings curled over her hands. When my mother's fury was spent, Augusta hit herself in the face as punishment or beat her own head with a coat hanger. Mother disappeared but Augusta remained there, and with tears in her eyes gazed at me and stroked my hands as if it were I who had to be consoled, and from a drawer in the kitchen table she took a dish of dessert, saved from mealtime. I went out into the street holding on to Augusta's hand. My exploration of the city is connected for me with the pressure of Augusta's hand. The streets rise in front of me with their creaking iron-rimmed wheels, with their haze of tar and malt and wet dust, with their warehouses at whose façades the chains of the hoists rattled, and in whose storerooms shapes moved about in the uncertain light between packing cases and sacks. We penetrated ever deeper into the alleyways, arcades, and tucked-away squares, past the soot-blackened, scaly, bescribbled masonry walls, until through gateway arches and down worn-out flights of steps we came to the dikes and onto the docks where the masts of ships stood out against the smoky sky, where watery reflections flickered on ships' sides, where black and yellow faces peered out of the round portholes and shouted out strange words, where the pennants buffeted on the taut rigging and screaking cargo cranes swung long necks around. Sometimes scenes from these wanderings suddenly surface in my dreams, first impressions which have preserved their glassy transparence and sharpness of focus, they show places, often without any recognizable happening, motionless and still, where I had suddenly become aware of my own existence. There is a broad, sandy avenue, the houses that flank it lie far back from the road, with steep steps leading up to the doors, and in the sand there are wheel tracks. Perhaps a car has just passed, but now the avenue is still and empty, and broods in the noonday warmth and is saturated with the momentousness and uniqueness of my existence. There is a street that slopes down from a rise; it is toward evening, colors shine out of the pinkly shimmering dusk. With long, high leaps, I go soaring down the street.

Behind the redly lustrous shutters I can make out carved figures of gods and elaborate model ships, chests with chased-silver locks, caskets inlaid with shells and pearls, silk handkerchiefs adorned with fire-breathing dragons, lacquered fans, reddish-gold bird feathers, and deep-blue butterflies, daggers with waved blades and ivory handles, a rusty pirate musket, nail-studded belts and riding boots with spurs, a white swan with outstretched neck, a horse's head with streaming mane, a naked blackblackwoman's body, pearl necklaces, bracelets, sawfish, alligators, and monkeys, and in the depths of a workshop, amid his leather stuff, Master Stahlhut at his last, mouth full of nails, hammering on a shoe sole with his hammer, warty face lit up by the glow from a crystal ball. I stood with Augusta on the bank of the river, a train of barges passed by, wash fluttering on one of the barges, and a small white, barking dog, and Augusta took a piece of chocolate from inside the crumbly black leather of her handbag and put it into my mouth. It tasted soapy from the inside of her bag. We stood in a tunnel, and over us rumbled a train and on the deep camber of the wall were stuck yellowed posters, blistered by paste, which Augusta murmuringly deciphered. We looked from all sides at the stone giant Roland in the marketplace and wondered what the dwarf might mean whose head and arms lay crushed between the giant's feet. Mother knew everything, could do everything, decided everything, but Augusta knew no more than I did and we looked at things with the same astonishment. We tried to explain to each other the snake gargoyles along the tops of the drainpipes, the figures of saints on the cathedral façade, the inscriptions on the doorways and the kings and knights mounted on their green-smudged horses, we puzzled and felt our way along passages and clumsily built-over courtyards, we saw the pigeons flying around the towers and followed the marching soldiers, keeping in time with their flashing, crashing instruments. Once, we found ourselves caught up in a crowd that had assembled in a square. All eyes were directed upward to a large house. High up on the walls a man was climbing. Someone said, Human fly. I asked Augusta what that was, a human fly. She did not know. It seemed to me some sort of profession, a rare and unusually difficult task to which one would have to devote the whole of one's life. I felt my palms beginning to sweat, I felt a fluttering in my stomach and in the bend of my knees, and a tickling on the soles of my feet, and I knew that this was all part of it. I realized that fear was the real motive for this performance, that one tried to overcome fear by the exertion of climbing. My encounter with the climber awakened in me the premonition of a vocation, it was as if I was looking ahead into my own future as, breathless and with fingers and toes tensed, I followed the movements of the man on the wall. At this moment, under a clear blue sky, out of which came the droning of a plane, light and metallic, the groundwork was laid of a longing to do something on my own. And so there was I, already involved in existence, already in the middle of life's committedness and so pushed on toward the barrel organ pipings and

the uproar of the fair, in a growing throng. The ground
was soft with confetti and paper streamers, in the booths
hot sausages, pretzels, and spun honey were being offered for sale, trumpet blares, shots and runs on the barrel organ became ever more piercing, elbows jogged me,
feet brushed against mine, and then everything was one
rotating movement of bodies, one vast bawling and
bubbling of voices, and I was part of it, was carried along
between the faces, hats, and arms, between the swaying
grape bunches of multicolored balloons, between the
large flopping streamers, between the wonderfully
painted whirring merry-go-rounds, and to the hoarse
question from the Punch and Judy show, Are you all
there, I answered yes in the chorus of countless voices,
and as Punch whacked at the policeman with his club, I
joined the collective shrieks of laughter, and I saw the
lady snake charmer on the platform in her tights of scintillating black scales and the largest man in the world
and the magician out of whose tailcoat pigeons flew and
everything was fleeting, everything changed form, and
the canvas of the tents billowed and whispered mysteriously in the wind, and the masks in the shooting galler-
ies jerked open their mouths, and on black cushions lay
golden medals, and over the rotating merry-go-round
hung clacking rings to be caught while in circling flight,
and in a miniature mine jerky little figures hacked at
tunnel walls, and cars drawn by stiff-legged horses
moved nearer along rails, and shovels were raised over
the cars, and away went the cars, and baskets sank down
through shafts, and cars inclined over baskets, and up

went the baskets and hung swinging over approaching
trains, and everything rattled and jerked until the mechanism suddenly fell silent and everything stopped in
mid-motion, cars stuck in the air with picks raised high,
horses frozen, baskets hanging still in the shaft, until
with a jerk everything got underway again, everything
moved along again, shook again, bobbed again, dragged
along again, hacked again, cracked again. And nearby
on a camp stool sat an old man with a white beard and a
broad-brimmed slouch hat, motionless and preoccu-
pied he leaned against his mechanical box, deaf to all the
questions one put to him. Amid a tangle of supporting
beams I climbed into a little roller-coaster car, and the
wild gay surge of life fell away behind me, ever farther I
drew away from the roar and the bustle, until all I could
hear was the rolling of the small, sturdy wheels on the
rails, and I was taken higher and higher till the highest
point was reached, from which I could look out far and
wide over the whole of the fairground and the city. The
car rested only a moment at its peak before it plunged
into the depths, but this moment was enough to transfix
me with an ecstatic feeling of liberty. There below me lay
the sea of roofs, with their smoking chimneys, there lay
the glittering water of the river, there lay the ships in the
harbor, the freighters and the great liners, there arched
the bridges with steaming trains, and on the towers the
light green copper shone and the golden weather vanes
flashed. Then came the downward plunge, down steep
run after run, around breathtaking curves, to the last
chasm with the pool where the water sprayed up around

the car as it shot through it. When it was dusk I drifted through the streets with the fair-day throng, swam slowly down the avenue with the crowd, saw above me the foliage of the trees glide back in autumnal gold, felt the wind on my perspiring forehead, held up before me the stick with the Chinese lantern in which a candle burned, and joined in the song that was always welling up in waves before and behind me, Lantern, lantern, sun, moon, and stars. And underneath the circus cupola a creature of the air lunged from trapeze to trapeze, turned a somersault, let out shrill, reckless cries, dived out of the heights at me with outspread arms, a precipitously flying mane of black hair, close in front of me she pulled herself out of her dive and drew herself up again, a breath of wind, filled with a curiously drugging fragrance, rushed past me. Her ecstatic smile in her golden-brown, slant-eyed face, her piercing bird cry, burned themselves into me forever. Soon, soon I would travel after her, would fly back and forth across the circus arena, soon, soon, only a short time off, I will belong to you, only first I have to learn to read and write, to get through school quickly, soon, soon, I shall be with you, and see your ecstatic smile again, and hear your wild cry. I learned writing with Berthold Merz in the shed next door in the courtyard of the slate factory, we scratched our first letters on black flat pieces from the scrap pile, and the sun shimmered through the cracks in the planks. Berthold's figure is fluid and fading, like dream figures in the morning shortly before waking, only his hand with the short stubby fingers and the bitten fingernails is clear. This hand grips the bow and shoots the arrow, the arrow with the feathered shaft, and the arrow rises high into the sky, so high that it disappears from our view and the arrow never returns. And Berthold Merz disappeared and Friederle took his place. A few years ago I stood in front of the house we had moved into at the time I was starting school. I had not seen the avenue for years, and now, seeing it again, I felt my childhood within me like the dull ache of an ulcer. The trunks of the trees at the side of the road had become strong and tall, the boughs spread far out over the road and their foliage closed together to form a thick canopy. Like someone entranced in an evil fairy tale I went toward the park to which the avenue led and in which our house lay hidden. On the pond at the edge of the avenue, a few white swans were swimming as before and in the hedge with the prickly leaves the white sweet peas bloomed as before. From the stream that separated the park from the avenue, I could see the house glinting bright red between the trees, it was intact, and in the adjoining garden lay the yellow villa in which Friederle had lived. Profound silence reigned, everything was steeped in its long past. In the muddy water of the brook a shoal of sticklebacks was flashing, tadpoles rowed with their tails around the algae, a frog with gaping eyes sat on the bank, a blue dragonfly whirred past. I went down the park path and stood still at the white posts of the garden gate in front of our house. The garden with its thicket of fir trees, its spreading copper beech and tall grass run wild extended to the elder bush at the edge of the fields. Beside the garden path lay the green hen-house, low and shrunken, and once we had jumped down from the dizzying heights of its skylight. The fenced-in hen yard was deserted, but a few white feathers still shone out of the dust. I asked a woman who came out of the house if she knew anything about the neighbors. She told me that out of the whole large family only one son was still alive, Friedrich, he had been an outstanding officer and had won the highest honors. He still lived in the town and she gave me his address. But I did not look him up, I knew what he was like. There stood Friederle at the fence of the neighboring garden, it was the day we moved in. He folded his arms and asked me imperiously what my name was. Are you going to live here, he asked, and I nodded and with my gaze followed the men who were carrying our furniture out of the moving van and into the house. Your house belongs to my father, Friederle said, you are only renting it. My father is a president, he said, what is your father. I did not know. What, you don't even know what your father is, he said. I sought for an answer that would overpower him, or win his favor, but I found none. Then he asked again. What's that you've got on your hat. I took the hat off. It was a sailor's hat with golden lettering on the headband. What is that, he asked again. I did not know. Can't you even read what's written on your own hat, he said. It says, I am stupid. And with that he took the hat from my hand and threw it high up into a tree. The hat stuck in the branches, the long blue ribbons fluttered in the wind. My mother came out onto the terrace of our house and saw us standing there side by side. Have you found a new playmate already, she cried. Are you having fun. Friederle pulled me with him into the depths of the garden, past the henhouse, from which we could hear a scratching and clucking, past the pump and the strawberry beds, through grass that grew up to our shoulders, through the shrubbery to the wet ditch that ran in a wide arc around our lot. There in front of us were the fields, the vast plain, over which the sun was burning down, the wind rushed toward us out of the open spaces and showered us with its pregnant odors of growing grain and clover and cow dung. Like a thin mist, the pictures of my old world were scattered and everything was clothed in blinding brightness. With the help of a stick, Friederle jumped over the ditch and signaled impatiently for me to follow. I threw myself across onto the bushy slope, skidded in the mud, pulled myself up by juicy, damp grasses, staggered out into the weight of a sea of air in which green plover were whistling past. And everything belonged to Friederle, he showed me the speckled birds' eggs in the dry, brittle sand, the bittercress with toad spit on it, molehills, field mice runs, foxholes, and then the hare. Do you see him, there, there, and I saw his white undertail disappearing in rapid zigzag leaps. He was always taking me into his domain, up to the marsh where the ground squished under our feet and where we sucked at the poisonous stalks of marsh marigolds. I went back by the avenue in the white dust of the roadway, my childhood lay decades behind me, I can depict it now with well-chosen words,

I can take it apart and spread it out in front of me, but as I experienced it, there was no thinking out and no dissecting, there was no controlling reason then, I was walking down the avenue and my black laced boots were whitened by the dust of the avenue, and Friederle walked beside me, and the white swans swam in the pond and in one garden a peacock strutted and opened up his scintillating fan of feathers, and it was the first day of school, from all directions children were streaming into school and each of them carried a little bag of candy to console him, and fear of the school was sticky and sickly with the taste of raspberry sweets. But in front of the school entrance I fled back, I raced back over the black cinders—trampled hard—of the playground, I ran back along the white dusty avenue, past the peacock and the swans, over the little bridge that led from the avenue into the park, into the overgrown depths of the park up to the edge of the fields, I can depict it now, see it all now, my first day at school, the beginning of my panic, I did not want to get caught, I fled, gasping, I struggled for breath, my throat and chest burned like fire, and so I stand at the edge of the fields and gradually my breathing grows calmer and I feel safe and for a while am free and away from all threats. Before me a wild rose bush grows, and in the thorns of the bush trembles a woolly tuft of hare's fur. Later that day, however, I was led back to school by my mother, later that day I stood with my mother in the corridor in front of the classroom door, and my mother knocked at the classroom door and the teacher opened the door from

within and inside all faces were turned toward me, all
within had formed a community together and I was the
one who had come too late. And every day I went down
the avenue with Friederle, and Friederle pressed against
me, dug his elbow into my side, shoved me to sidewalk
edge. I avoided him and walked in the road. Why don't
you walk here beside me, Friederle asked, and made
room for me. Hardly had I started walking next to him
when he rammed his elbow into my ribs again. I began
to run, but he held me back by my satchel. We came to
the square where the street to school forked off, and
Friederle stuck his leg between mine so that I fell, my
satchel sprang open, books spilled out, the slate and the
box of chalk clattered out, the box with my sponge in it
rolled far away over the cobbles up to the tramcar conductors who here, at the end of the line, were sitting on
the trolley car steps, eating their breakfast and laughing
and munching their sandwiches, the conductors threw
the box across to me, it was a box made of black lacquered wood, with a red rose painted on it. Here at the
square where the road to school branched off, a whole
enchanting world began, walls of fortresslike buildings
pushed close together, with glimpses of courtyards and
stables, a church tower built of rough stone rose up out
of the shingled roofs, in a wheel at the top of the spire
storks had made their nest and struck out at one another
with their long, sharp beaks. Behind the leaded panes of
a window sat an aged man in a rocking chair, and out of
a gatehouse came two men with knives, their faces taut
and reddish and silkily shining like the thin skin over

healing wounds, and behind them on a heap of brush-
wood lay a pig, its four legs bound together, and on a
red-tiled wall a butterfly trembled with outspread wings
that had black and yellow markings, and a hand holding
a needle thrust out between its fingers approached the
butterfly and the needle pierced it through. On the
school playground rose a small stone building with an
arched, shabby doorway, and when one pressed one's
eyes to the windowpanes and shielded them from the
sides with one's hands, one could see inside in the half
dark the carriage with its high, turned doorposts and
black canopy and it sometimes happened that the coach-
man came in a long frock coat with his big black horse,
cautiously opened the door, backed the horse into the
shafts, and drove the creaking carriage out. The piercing
bell summoned us to the classrooms. Here was a whirring and stirring up of dust around the splintery desks
that smelled of ink and cold sweat. I unpacked the slate
and the broken chalk. Friederle turned around in his
place and threatened me with his fist. The teacher called
me out to the front. I had not understood his question, I
never understood his questions. His bloated face rocked
close in front of me, his eyes bulged at me, his thick lips
opened. Now, what was it I wanted, he asked, and rubbed
my ear with the knuckles of his clenched fist, and white
threads of saliva trembled on his opened lips. From the
benches all around me came a tittering. Even the
teacher's face was distorted into a grin. That they all
laughed at me was proof that I was funny, and so I too
grinned, and this ability to amuse others was a valuable

gift. But, the teacher screamed, you're still laughing, and
his grin had only been a baring of his teeth, and the
laughter around me from the benches oozed away. I was
hauled up by the ear onto the podium and placed in
front of the blackboard, and what I had to demonstrate
to the teacher and class was how one kept one's palm
held out under the raised cane. It was a difficult exercise,
for my hand would not stay still under the cane, it always jerked back. The class was one, single, thick, blood-
thirsty silence. The teacher took aim and swished the
cane down and my hand drew back, and the stroke
whistled through the air. And the teacher shouted,
What, trying to duck your punishment, are you, and
snatched my hand up again and once more swished the
cane down at me, again my hand drew back and again it
was held up, and the cane came down again, and again
my hand drew back, and again it was held up, and again
the cane whistled down until finally it caught my hand
and the smarting weal spread out over my palm. Blinded
by welling tears, gripping the wrist of my aching hand
with the other hand, I stumbled back to my place. Thus
it was that I learned in school how to hold out my hand
for the teacher's cane. And after school I tried to evade
Friederle, but with his gang of cronies he hunted me out
everywhere. When I ran they ran along beside me.
When I walked slowly they walked slowly beside me.
When I dodged suddenly to the other side of the street
they threw stones at me. These small whistling stones,
and the mocking voices over there, how well they knew
that I was a fugitive, that I was in their power. And my

little subterfuges, suddenly I bent double and raised my hand to my forehead, screaming as if I had been hit. That alarmed my pursuers and they cravenly slunk away, but I was more cowardly for I knew that if they now felt guilty they would later only punish me the more, so I shouted after them, You didn't mean me, it was a mistake, you meant someone else. After lunch, between two and three, as I lay on my bed resting, a lostness came over me. I lay motionless and held my breath. If I only lay long enough without breathing, I could forget the breathing altogether. Then, like a stone in water, I sank, and soft, black rings spread out above me. But suddenly I hit the ground and, shaken by the jolt, was wrenched back to the surface. Now everything in me became large and swollen and inflated, I became a giant, an all-powerful being, and stretched out on the yellow desert of the blankets I played with little colored grains of sugar that I had scraped off a piece of chocolate. The grains trickled around under my hands, grains like heaps of people seen from a vast distance. I blew into the motley heap of people and they scattered in wild flight. The giant is coming, the giant is coming, they shouted below in the desert, and the earth rumbled under the giant's steps, the giant appeared on the horizon, the ingeniously constructed giant, a thousand stories high, populated by workers who serviced the heating system and the machinery, the electricity circuits and switchboards in the interior, and controlled by technicians and officers in the center of the globe of the head, in the eye chambers, the brain halls, the canals of the nostrils, the eardrums.

I myself was the commander in chief over this metallic structure in human form, I issued my orders through megaphones, and I was responsible for seeing that all the joints and limbs moved according to plan and that balance was kept at the vast speed at which it jerked itself forward. Jungles crumpled like stubble under the robot's feet, with a single leap he sprang over the widest rivers, the highest mountains, the oceans were puddles to him, and his head disappeared in the clouds. Then I heard Tarmina outside in the garden calling my sisters. I ran to the window, saw Tarmina with upturned face among the rhododendron bushes, Tarmina Nebeltau in her pink dress with the silk ribbon in her hair. I ran downstairs, Margit and Irene came too, we fluttered around the garden, to the swing, the sandpit, the ditch, we trampled the tall grass down into paths, hid ourselves from each other, looked for each other. Then in the wood, to the witches and the will-o'-the-wisps. Ran on the soft springy carpet of pine needles, looked into the hollow trunk where the owl lived, started up rabbits in their runs, chased after the dragonflies by the pond, heard the cuckoo calling from the trees how many years we still had to live. Found in the grass the blue and white feather of a jay and gave it to Tarmina, who stroked herself with it on her closed eyelids. In a clearing I saw Tarmina dancing with Margit, Irene called after them and they rushed toward her, the branches they brushed past in their haste still swung as their steps faded away into the rustling foliage. This clearing, reached by a grass path, lies there in its glittering insistence, a milky blue light hovers over the green green grass that has been stamped down by the dancers' feet. Then back to the garden. Friederle, with a flushed face, called me over to the copper beech at the top of which he had built a lookout. We clambered up and saw far away on the horizon a factory erupt in flames and smoke, then we let ourselves drop backward, stretched out flat, springing from bough to bough. Friederle and my sisters disappeared in the tall grass. Alone with Tarmina beside the swing. Tarmina in front of me on the seat of the swing, swaying lightly away from me, toward me, the air heavy with the scent of lilac. Then suddenly she bends forward as she comes toward me, and kisses me on the mouth. She glides back again, jumps off the swing, and runs away. The kiss on my lips, the empty swing, swinging to and fro, Tarmina near me a moment ago, now with the others, did not again turn around to me. She disappeared with Friederle in the tall grass. Instead of going after her, instead of winning her for myself, I crept back into the house. The kitchen was empty, all the rooms were empty. Only Augusta was upstairs in her attic room. I went over to Augusta's chest of drawers and took in my hand the round, white sea-smoothed and polished stone that she kept there, folded my hand over it, held it, felt the inside of my hand quite filled with it, and asked Augusta if she would put a disk in the music box. Augusta wound up the machine with the key. While the brittle, cracked melody trickled out of the indented tin plate, Augusta with the veined hands folded sat in her violet slip at the edge of the bed, and through the open window I heard from afar the rolling of the trains and the voices of the children playing in the garden. From Augusta's room it was only a few steps to the attic, a large room supported by wooden posts where the warmth pressed down on one, sultry and motionless, while beneath its round gable windows the floor lay full of dead wasps. The place of exile that I had found in the summer house continued in this attic. In the sensual pleasure of a secret search, I opened suitcases and chests in which things out of my parents' past were kept, I lifted out a light gray uniform that my father had worn during the war, I spread out the uniform on the floor, laid the saber next to it, the saber with the silver tassel at the handle and the field glasses he had carried in the battle in which he was wounded. They were said to have saved his life, for the focusing screw was smashed flat and had softened the impact of the bullet that had penetrated his body. Black-rimmed bullet holes could still be seen in the leather case. Next to my father's uniform I laid out an expensive dress of my mother's, a fan of ostrich feathers, a pearl-inlaid diadem. This was the reconstruction of a prehistoric moment. Full of uneasiness and suspense I tried to find out something about my origins. About my father I knew nothing. The strongest impression he made was his always being away somewhere. I had heard only a few words about his past. My grandfather had a long white beard, he used to say. Or, I went into business when I was very young and supported my family. In the rare hours of mutual understanding, on a Sunday or on Christmas Eve, he used to tell me how when I was still small he used to let me ride on his knee and how I always wanted to hear the story that he told me then, and now, playing with his saber in the loft, I sang this story to myself, Once there was a little boy, who climbed an apple tree, along came a man with a big sword, and the man shouted, You better get right down out of that apple tree, and the boy fell out of the tree. I could still remember how in that dark earlier time the knee pulled away from under me to one side, and I slid into the depths, held back by my father's hands. Of my mother I knew that before she married my father she had been an actress. The costumes in the suitcases derived from that period, and little boxes were filled with photographs on which she could be seen as an Egyptian princess, an abbess, a gypsy woman, and a Greek priestess. Another picture showed her with my stepbrothers and her first husband, who wore a big, bristly mustache. On the basis of vague hints that I had heard about him, I imagined him as a thug and a sex maniac. He looked like my mother's father, who appeared in another picture. At the dinner table this father used to keep a dog whip beside him with which he gave his six daughters cracks over the head, and made them, as they sat, keep newspapers tucked under their arms to learn perfect posture. I am grateful to him for this strict bringing-up, my mother said, it has made me strong. From the fragments I found in the attic, I was able to piece together a family history. There were photos of my father at an equator-crossing ceremony on board a ship going to South America, there was the engagement photograph with my father in

uniform, arm in arm with my mother. He was lean, delicately built, my mother large and stately in a dress that
reached to the ground. My mother liked telling us the
story of their first meeting, it was the romance of the
little lieutenant who wooed the celebrated actress and
showered her with flowers and finally won her. It was a
story not to be fathomed, quite as impenetrable as it is
today as I brood over those personal documents of my
parents that had been saved from destruction. Why did
my mother give up the theater. Did not her later lack of
stability come from her having forsaken the career she
was naturally cut out for. She did not like the world of
the theater any more, she said, it was too free and easy,
life in it too makeshift. She created the elegant and the
grand in her own home, the large receptions, the extravagance, the expensive clothes, all these became her
substitute for the roles she might have played on the
stage. My researches in the attic are supplemented today by a letter that my father wrote my mother before
the battle in which he received his stomach wound. The
contents of the letter are as follows, Zaklikow, 5th July
1915. In the event of my being killed in battle, I request
whoever finds me to send the enclosed letter to Frau XX
by the quickest possible way, and furthermore to inform
the same by telegram of my death. Please also send the
ring on my finger, together with all my papers, to the
same Frau XX. All other objects, such as my linen, clothing, and equipment, may be disposed of among such of
my comrades as need them. Any cash remaining after
deductions for postage expenses may likewise be

distributed among my companions. If possible also inform the aforementioned person where I am buried. With many thanks for any trouble the carrying out of my requests may have caused you. Then the letter to my mother, My dearest wish was to return home once more from the war, to return to you, my beloved. If it is not granted me to see you again, these lines that I write before going into battle will greet you for the last time. It is difficult for me to imagine that I shall no longer see your dear eyes nor feel your lips, that your arms will no longer enfold me. If I were still alive your life would only just have begun, I should have arranged everything more beautifully than you could have ever dreamed of, my life too would only just be beginning. The will, of which you have a copy, is deposited with the lawyer. See to it also, please, that the balance sheet is audited at M's, and then I wanted to say to you that my, that is my heirs', profit-sharing in the business continues for another year. The articles in my apartment are all at your disposal. And the ring you gave me that I am now wearing, I hope you get it back. Never give it to anyone else. And now farewell, my beloved, I shall kiss you to my last breath. Reading this letter brings back to me my eavesdropping in the nights of my childhood when I lay awake with my ear pressed to the wall to catch something of the distant, murmuring voices of my parents. This eavesdropping, this groping, this concealment upstairs in the sultry attic. The battlefield. The shots of the machine gun. My father in a foxhole. My father with a bleeding stomach, moaning among other wounded in the field hospital. And then my mother appearing. She finds him in this field hospital, in this overcrowded, stinking ward where he lies bleeding. She carries him out in order to look after him herself. In the picture world of my mythology she holds him in her arms, she carries him along a sodden and rutted track, above her the torn, low-flying clouds. Columns of soldiers, cannons come toward her, the wind rushes through the willows. This retrospective brooding and fantasy-making, this expectant eavesdropping, this suspense came before the secret games that were the real reason for my visits to the attic. Filled with the certainty of being completely secluded and forgotten by everyone, I stole away to my model countryside which I had built on a plank from clay and sand and stones and moss. When I lowered my face to the edge of the countryside it was as if I were there myself, reconnoitering, and my watchful gaze lit upon hills, woodlands, ditches and gullies and trenches and drawn-up cannons and the General Staff in a council of war and everything held its breath, everything waited for the explosion. With a cold passion I marked off the countryside, arranged the positions of the troops, built up the fortresses, made a gully steeper, put in another thicket, and only when I was finished with every detail and the total impact of the work satisfied me did I move on to the actual combat. The battle broke out. Soldiers stormed out of their trenches, the cannons opened up their bombardment. After every hurricane of annihilation that I let loose over the landscape, I scrutinized the resulting situation from all angles, in close-up I saw

the dead and wounded half buried in shell craters and
uprooted woods, the fallen horses and smashed cannons in the ruins of castles, saw soldiers lying on top of
each other in a cruel wrestling match, saw troops lurking in ambush. Again new waves of attacks broke loose,
crowned by the holocaust. The copse, the fences, the
bridges, the melting dugouts turned to charcoal, soldiers collapsed, the colors ran off them like blood and
mud, and I drank in the visions of my passing world,
breathed in the stench of molten tin and burned wood
until nothing existed any longer but one single smolder-
ing desolation. After the great battles when the mangled
corpses had been buried and the wounded had been
brought to the field hospitals, I made little expeditions,
in which only a few specially privileged figures took
part. These expeditions were marked by a sense of relief
and a desire to explore. With these figures I crossed the
broad sweep of the floor, landed with them on foreign
shores, reached inaccessible mountain peaks or distant
planets. But always I had to return to my battleground
on the board and had to recompose my landscape and
populate it with troops. High up in our house I spread
death and destruction all about me. Something incomprehensible had begun within me. I sought release. But
in the evenings the incomprehensible came and paralyzed me. I hid my hands under the blanket. But my
mother would come and lift out my hands again. Imperiously she pressed my hands down onto the blanket.
My hands had to lie outside in the cold, exposed to
ghostly attackers. Cramped in fear I lay, abandoned to

visions of giants and huge animals. I stared into the twilight of the room that became ever more inky until the
objects in it began to dissolve into black floating patches,
I strained my eyes to the utmost to find something recognizable and things moved everywhere in the shadows, in the shadows the figures squatted and lurked,
they crept out from behind the curtain, they rose up
from the floor with a soft crackling and whistling. Sweat
streamed down over me. The attacks had hardly begun
but I was already annihilated. I did not move, so as not
to attract the attention of the ghosts. I held my breath,
only my heart hammered, and now it came toward me
from all sides, I pretended to be dead, if only my heart
would not thud so, I lay amid crouching nameless things
that were plotting to murder me. I could not scream, I
tried frantically to force out some sound but I didn't
succeed, it was as if I no longer knew my own voice, how
I could ever make it come out again, only after complete
exhaustion did a strangled sound come out, which hung
in the room and balled itself together, to come at me
again. Every night I died, strangled, suffocated. Still,
sometimes, after reaching insensibility, I succeeded in
getting beyond fear, in breaking through horror once it
had reached its utmost power, whereupon I got out of
bed, the horror having changed into a voluptuous
weightlessness, on tiptoe I glided through the room,
opened the door, jumped over the large yellow lion that
lay in front of my door and with floating steps, which
seemed nevertheless to be held back by some tough,
slimy resistance, moved along the corridor to the door

of my parents' bedroom. It was an endlessly long corridor, behind me loomed the stairs up to the attic and
beside me stretched the banisters, below which lay the
dark shaft of the stairway down to the entrance hall, in
front of me, in the niche next to my parents' bedroom, a
few wicker chairs stood softly creaking and crackling,
the white parts of their flower-patterned cushions standing out sharply in the darkness. From below came the
slow, heavy ticking of the grandfather clock, slow, heavy
steps came up the stairs, it was the Sandman coming
with his sack of sand. Beyond the window lay the garden
plunged in deepest violet, the window was open, the
garden stretched and breathed, and from the ditch I
caught the half-extinguished cries of a drowning child.
The door to my parents' bedroom stood ajar, I cautiously
pushed it open and entered. In their double bed, which
stood at right angles to the wall and protruded into the
middle of the room, lay my parents, on the left my father
snoring softly and on the right my mother, her face
framed by the darkness of her hair. Both lay on their
backs, and above them, on the wall at the head of the
bed, hung three pictures, on the left a painting of my
father's face, the head, in the oval of the cardboard
mount, looking like a head cut off, to the right a repro-
duction of a picture of a naked youth, seen in profile,
who with his arms around his knees and his face resting
on his knees sat high up above a desolate mountain
landscape, and in the middle the picture of the naked
goddess, who, surrounded by foam, bent stiffly forward,
without ever losing her balance, covering her breasts

with one hand and with the other clasping a strand of
her long, flowing hair in front of her genitals, stood on
the rim of a huge shell. The clothes lay carefully folded
on the chairs next to the bedside tables on my father's
side and on my mother's side, and beneath the chairs the
shoes stayed close together like patiently waiting animals. In the mirror of the large wardrobe on the wall
opposite the bed, I saw myself, saw myself in the violet
moonlight in the depths of the transfigured room. My
parents tried, on our family doctor's advice, to put an
end to my nocturnal wanderings, they surrounded my
bed with large basins of water that were to wake me
from my somnambulant state when I stepped into them.
This treatment resulted in my learning to fly. I increased
the horror and the creepiness by artificially induced
cold shivers that had the property of making me weight-
less and with their help, stretched out stiff, I hovered up
out of bed, to fly, feet first and flying on my back, straight
across the room, through the open window and over the
garden. I steered myself with light movements of my
hands and toes, feeling triumphantly happy, lowering
and raising myself according to the varying degrees of
my cold shivers. I passed so close by the top of the copper beech that its soft warm leaves brushed me. These
nocturnal excursions were the preliminaries to severe
attacks of fever which for a long while, at intervals of
two weeks or so, overcame me for some days at a time.
A committee of doctors stood around my bed, removed
their glittering pince-nez, tugged thoughtfully at their
beards, tested my pulse, pressed hairy middle fingers

into my stomach, knocked with bent index fingers on my chest, telephoned to my heart, hit my knee with little silver hammers, and could find nothing to explain my symptoms. Finally the theory was put forward that a fly had carried bacilli to me from the malaria cultures of a nearby mental hospital. The chain of thought that attributed the origins of my illness to a mental hospital made me think that I must be near to madness, I studied my face in the mirror, made faces, babbled foolishness and let my spittle drip out of my mouth as I had seen happen at times with the mental defectives I had watched on their walks in the park. I learned to live in that way, I know that something is missing, I fumble about and search, I whimper and scream and I don't find it, I grow, I develop, and my freedom of movement is ever more restricted, I scarcely dare look any longer, everywhere I knock against boundaries, and creep off to hide. I learn to fly and I learn how to catch fevers. I make myself at home in the great lack, in the disease of disappointment, of impotence and mistrust. And deep down in me the unsatisfied wish lived on. When my mother, summoned by my scream, came to my bed and set me upright and enclosed me in her arms, the sinister atmosphere to which her own appearance had contributed vanished. It was she who threatened me, but at the same time she was my savior. She took away with one hand and gave back with the other, and thus kept me in continual suspense, almost as if I longed for the eerie, as if I found a certain enjoyment in its torments because I could afterward savor the relief. Only once in my

childhood had I experienced a foretaste of bodily freedom. I was with my parents and brothers and sisters on
a visit to a family with whom we were on friendly terms,
Fritz W., our host, was in every way my father's opposite.
He was strong and lively, he had a witty and direct way
of speaking, he was comradely in the way he treated his
children and intimate and demanding in his approach
to my mother, who blossomed in his company. I per-
ceived clearly the rivalry that arose between him and
my father, with Fritz the contest was relaxed and self-
confident whereas with my father it expressed itself in
strained self-control. Fritz's children jumped around the
garden naked, two girls and a boy, the same age as I and
my two younger sisters. We were in our Sunday best and
looked on in embarrassment at the naked, sun-burned
bodies at their play. My sisters wore white frocks with
starched collars, white knee stockings, and buckled
shoes. I had on my dark blue sailor suit, with the thickly
knotted tie, also white stockings and black laced boots.
It was midsummer. Then Fritz suddenly leaped at us,
and in a few tugs ripped my sisters' clothes off, I myself
crept under the low branches of a fir tree, but he pulled
me out into the open, stripped off my trousers and
blouse and shoved me together with my sisters into the
circle of his own children. In dismay we fumbled off the
remainder of our clothing and felt the warm air on
the whole of our skin. My parents had got up from their
garden chairs and were completely overcome by what
was happening. And we now found out what we could
have found out any day that summer, though it never

returned, how alive we became in our nakedness. We
felt the grass, leaves, earth, and stones with all our pores
and nerves, romping and shouting with joy, we lost ourselves in a brief dream of unsuspected potentialities. On
one other occasion Fritz W. intervened in my life. It was
years later. I came home with my school report, which
contained one terrible sentence, in face of which my
whole being seemed to crumble. I made great detours
with this sentence, did not dare go home with it, always
looked to see if it had not suddenly disappeared, but it
was still there, clear and distinct. When I finally reached
home, because I did not have the courage to ship out as
cabin boy to America, Fritz W. was sitting with my parents. What's that glum face for, he called out to me. Is it
a bad report card, my mother asked in her concerned
voice and my father looked toward me as if he saw all
the troubles of the world piling up behind me. I passed
the report to my mother, but Fritz snatched it out of my
hand and read it and broke into peals of laughter. Not
promoted, he cried, and slapped himself on the thighs
with his powerful hand. Not promoted, he shouted
again, while my parents looked in consternation first at
him, then at me, then he drew me to him and slapped
me on the shoulder. Not promoted, just like me, he said,
I stayed in the same class four times, all gifted men have
had to repeat classes at school. With that my deathly
anxiety dissolved, all danger passed. No longer could
my parents' shocked faces work themselves into a rage,
no longer could they reproach me with anything, for
after all Fritz W., this hard-working and successful man,

had removed all stigma from me and even thought me
worthy of special honor. These two encounters with
Fritz W. were the highlights of my childhood, for they
showed me how different the course of my life could
have been under other circumstances, and they showed
me the wealth of unexpended happiness that was in me
and still lies within me beneath the boils and matted
hair. When my puberty began, my mother again forced
me onto the white guitar-shaped sacrificial bowl on
which I had already sat in Green Street, this time to
clean my penis. With soap, warm water, and cotton wool
my mother tried to force back the foreskin, one hand
holding my genitals, while the other pressed and urged
the all too tight skin. I had half fainted with pain and
humiliation by the time the tip of my penis was laid bare
and my mother had washed away the smegma that had
collected under the foreskin. Later I asked her what it
was, the white slime that sometimes leaked out of me at
night, I knew well enough, but I wanted to provoke her,
by pretending ignorance I taunted her, and she answered, that's dirt, you must keep yourself clean, abso-
lutely clean, the dirt comes from all those dirty thoughts
you have. For a long time I could not rid myself of the
feel of her hand grasping my penis. In bed of an evening
it twitched and reared up, it throbbed and swelled up
and burned. A furious hatred of this organ seized me, I
would have liked to chop it off, but the voluptuousness
that accompanied these painful movements increased
and I gave way to them even if as a result of this surren-
der my hair and my teeth should fall out and my face be

covered with boils. This alloy of pain and pleasure set its
stamp on the fantasies of my dissipations. I imagined
myself imprisoned by violent, barbaric women who
bound me and overwhelmed me with their cruel caresses. You need more fresh air, people said, when they
noticed my hollow eyes, you need exercise and company. And so I was given a uniform, a neckerchief, a
shirt with a fleur-de-lis badge on the breast pocket, a
peaked hat, a knapsack, and a jackknife, and I was sent
off with marching groups into the countryside. In the
evenings Abi, the leader, crept under the blanket with
me at the hostel and asked me if I wanted to be his adju-
tant. He embraced me with his hairy arms and legs, his
bristly chin roamed over my face and his thick, red lips
tried to kiss my mouth. I turned away from him but the
voluptuous nauseating dream continued. We climbed
naked in the trees, not in free, animal-like nakedness,
but in a frantic feverish nakedness, we emptied our se-
men into the rough bark of the trees, we whipped each
other with switches and wrestled with one another in
burning lasciviousness in the moist warm earth, we bur-
rowed our way through the woods, built shelters, stayed
overnight in barracks where we learned to handle machine guns, and in the realization of my old war games I
took part in an attack on the camp of an enemy group,
we rushed out of our ambush over to their tents, plun-
dered and sacked them, then as quick as lightning disappeared again into the woods. Close in front of me I
still see the frightened face of a boy from whom, despite his pleadings, I wrested a carved staff, and then

possessed with the flush of victory rushed off with my loot. Like an evil omen this crying terror-stricken face now rose up in front of me, I felt that somewhere I was doing violence to myself, but I did not perceive it, I was caught up by a whirling hurricane. Everything was inflated and swollen. As I had myself been courted so now I courted another, moodily he let himself be kissed by me, then deceived me, looked from his embracing smilingly over to me, threw back his head with its long black hair and shut his eyes. Everything was filled with furtive enticements, advances, jealousies, and slanderings. Favorites were played off one against the other, and ingenious punishments devised for the scapegoats. All the destructiveness and lust for power in us was allowed to unfold. I became Friederle. I was there when a weak one was dragged to the stove and made to kiss the hot iron, I was there when we pushed a prisoner off on a raft on a flooded building site and pelted it with lumps of clay, I was filled with brief happiness to be able to be one of the strong ones, although I knew that my place was among the weaklings. As the sly and treacherous and sinister elements within us grew, we began to throw our weight about in the streets, fires were started, shop windows smashed, passersby were knocked down and flags were borne past to sarcastic cries of Hats off. Contorted in a cramp of reverence we sang the national anthem and heaven help him who did not bare his head. In the evenings in the blossoming avenues I swept out on my bicycle after the girls. But it seemed impossible ever to touch these shrinking figures with their darkly giggling

voices. Unattainable, I saw the brightness of their dresses
dissolve into the depths of the leaf-shaded streets, dazed
by the heavy scent of the blossom I heard soft steps beside me, heard the whispering of a tender voice in my
ear, and ever more deeply I gave myself up to the hallu-
cinations of the night till a dream being rose at my side,
until I saw a face next to me, a face without features, a
face that was a conglomeration of my own feelings, and
I caressed this face, this face of self-love, no other face
existed, thus I had to invent one, I kissed this face, I
kissed the air, I kissed myself reeling under my need for
love, and everything sank from me, the pressure of
school, the threats and warnings, and I heard the de-
mands of the world now only as a distant eternal surge.
And I changed even this surge to my own purposes. In
the evenings, alone in my room, a wild sea surrounded
the island on which I lived with my beloved, here the
waves had tossed us up onto the beach, and here we
dwelt between the cliffs in a tumbledown hut, entirely
given up to our mad love. It was complete love, herma-
phroditic love, enclosed in itself, and self-consuming.
My beloved was part of me, she was the female element
in me, I knew every one of her movements, and she re-
sponded to every one of my movements. When I embraced her I embraced myself, offered myself, pressed
into myself. And then, after the spilled happiness, the
room resumed its shape, the terribly same old room,
and destroyed my imaginings. The dream scattered like
ashes and I lay and listened to the ticking of the clock
in the hall. This wakeful loneliness was part of our

encounters, this was the price, that I had to lie awake a long time, with aching eyes, in a slow dying, in a slow inward decay. But next morning my longing for a new meeting made itself felt again and I waited impatiently for the evening. In the lethargic hour between two and three I lay on the sofa in the living room, with my hands folded under my head, staring up at the color print of Hannibal's Tomb on the wall. Beneath a grayish brown, massive, many-branched tree there rose a heap of stones, next to which stood an old shepherd, leaning contemplatively on his crook, while before him a flock of sheep grazed in the wild, dry grass. The window onto the street stood open, outside motes of white sunlight danced, and from the tennis court on the opposite side of the road sounded the heavy, dull thuds of the ball being hit. Occasionally right beneath my window a car hummed past, or a bicycle bell rang. The thought of the city outside put new life into me, I saw in front of me the long, broad blocks of streets, the giant houses borne up by bent stone slaves, the castles, museums, monuments, and towers, the overhead railways on their viaducts and the underground railways with their bustling crowds and their rattling advertisement boards. I was about to get up when I saw my mother standing in front of me, I never noticed how she got into the room, she always appeared suddenly in the middle of the room as if she had grown out of the ground, dominating the room with her omnipotence. Have you done your homework, she asked, and I sank back into my weariness. Once again she asked, Have you already finished your homework.

Out of my indifference I answered, I'll do it later. But she shouted, You'll do it now. I'll do it afterward, I said in a feeble attempt at defiance. Now she raised her fist, as in a coat of arms, and shouted her heraldic motto: I won't put up with contradiction. She stepped up close to me and her words fell onto me like stones. You must plug and plug away, you will have a few years, then you'll go out into life and for that you've got to be able to do something, otherwise you'll go to rack and ruin. She pulled me to the desk, to the schoolbooks. You are not to let me down, she said, I suffer sleepless nights because of you, I'm responsible for you and if you're a failure, it will reflect on me. Life means working, working, and then more working. Then she left me alone, next to me on a board stood a model city that I had constructed out of paper and cellophane, wires and rods. After my destructive games this was the first attempt to be constructive. It was a city of the future, a utopian metropolis, but it was incomplete, a mere skeleton, and I suddenly knew that I would not build at it any further, I saw only crumpled and glue-cracked paper, and everything was bent out of shape and fragile, one could blow it over with a single breath. I had to look for other means of expression. While I was brooding over my diary the door opened and my father entered. He saw me crouching over my desk busy with something in which he was never allowed to share, he saw how something quickly disappeared into the drawer. What are you up to over there, he asked. I'm doing my homework, I said. Yes, that is what I wanted to discuss with you, he said. There was an embarrassing tension, as always with such discussions. You are old enough now, he said, for me to be able to discuss the problem of a career with you. What do you think you'd really like to do. I could not answer this painful question. With a voice that was meant to sound understanding, and had something of the man-to-man chat about it, he said, I suggest you go to Commerce High and then come into my office. I murmured something about wanting first to finish school, in this way I could at least gain time. My father said now with growing impatience, You don't seem capable of doing that. I don't believe you are talented enough for that, and as for studying you haven't got the stamina, no, you ought to be doing some practical work. His face was gray and careworn. When one talks about life, one has to be gray and careworn. Life means seriousness, effort, responsibilities. My face, the face of a dunce and a loafer, twisted into an embarrassed stereotyped grin. In a hurt voice my father said, You don't need to laugh, life's not a laughing matter and it's about time that you learned how to work properly. Perhaps he felt a twinge of tenderness for me, but when he saw my averted, hostile look, he had to make himself hard and show me how firm his will. With the palm of his hand he hit the table and cried out, When this school year is over, we'll put an end to your daydreaming, then you'll have to come to terms with the realities of life. The realities of life. On my father's lips, these realities became a term for all that was sterile and petrified. I had already lost a decade in this reality, in the domain of school, where during endless hours my senses had been deadened. The threat that I should have to go out into life meant merely a continuation of my long wandering through classrooms and echoing corridors. There, after all, we had been prepared, for proficiency and responsibility, as it was called, by teachers whose spirits had given out. These long stony passages, in which rows of animal-smelling raincoats hung, while from within behind the doors I heard the litany of the school children from which occasionally one single voice would ring out high and clear, these stony passages, paced by the all-seeing Headmaster under whose annihilating gaze I sank onto my knees, these stony passages, among the flagstones throughout which fossils were interspersed, millions of years old, shaped like comets. From here I was supposed to go on into the corridors of office blocks, to the filing cabinets, the clatter of typewriters, into the rooms where the business affairs of this world were handled. But I had found other things in my search for nourishment for my expanding needs, things that gave me answers to my questions, words of poetry that suddenly stilled my restlessness, pictures that took me up into them, music that touched an answering chord within me. In books I encountered the life that school had kept hidden from me. In books I was shown another reality of life than that into which my parents and teachers wanted to force me. The voices of books demanded my collaboration, the voices of books demanded that I open myself up and reflect upon myself. I hunted through my parents' library. I was forbidden to read these books, so I had to remove them secretly and carefully even out the gaps, my reading took place at night under the blankets by flashlight, or on the toilet seat, or camouflaged behind schoolbooks. The chaos within me of half-baked longings, of romantic extravagances, of terrors and wild dreams of adventure, was reflected back at me in countless mirrors, I preferred the seamy, the suggestive, the lurid, I sought after sexual descriptions, devoured the stories of courtesans and clairvoyants, of vampires, criminals, and libertines, and like a medium I found my way to the seducers and fantasts and listened raptly to them in my inner confusion and melancholy. But the more I became aware of myself, and the less I shrank back from myself, the stronger became my desire for the voice of the book to speak to me in the plainest terms and conceal nothing from me. Soon I could tell the character of the narration from the first words of a book. I wanted it to excite me straightaway, I wanted to feel its glow and inner conviction at once. Long descriptive passages made me impatient. I wanted to be drawn into the middle of things right from the very start, and to know at once what it was about. I read poems only rarely, for here everything was too highly wrought, too much subject to a formal framework. I distrusted well-rounded and perfected things and I found it tiresome to search for the hidden meaning beneath all the artistry and polish. Often the well-planned work of art left me cold while the raw and only half formed caught hold of me. My logical thinking was underdeveloped. When I tried to counteract this lack by reading scientific or philosophic works, the

letters blurred before my eyes, I could not piece ι.
together into living words, I felt no breath in them.
What I retained belonged less to the realm of general
knowledge than to that of sensations, my knowledge
was composed of picturelike experiences, of memories
of sounds, voices, noises, movements, gestures, rhythms,
of what I had fingered or sniffed, of glimpses into rooms,
streets, courtyards, gardens, harbors, workshops, of vibrations in the air, of the play of light and shadow, of the
movements of eyes, mouths, and hands. I learned that
beneath logic there was another form of consistency, the
consistency of inexplicable impulses; here I discovered
my own nature, here in what was apparently unorga-
nized, in a world that did not obey the laws of the external order. My thinking allowed no particular goal, but
drove me from one to the other, tolerated no superim-
posed guidelines, often threw me into pitfalls and
abysses from which no explanations but only secret, unexpectedly discovered paths could guide me out again.
In the course of years the dialogue I sought for in books,
in ever more decisive and immediate form, turned ever
more deeply toward the personal sphere, and thus it became an ever rarer experience, for only a few could ex-
press some part of the things that touched the roots of
being. All stages of my development have their own
books. In Green Street there was a big book bound in
yellow hardboard with the corners all nicked off and in
it the adventures of little Mucki were reported. Mucki is
a great hero, it said, he knocks off the heads of thistles
in the field. I see him before me, Mucki in his baggy

cowboy trousers with leather fringes, with a broad-brimmed sombrero and a lasso, surrounded by cacti and rattlesnakes. Mucki was my first alter ego, in the malicious expression on his face was revealed what had been so well covered up in my own appearance, in him I could give full vent to my suppressed aggressiveness, Mucki the adventurer and gangster who was much more myself than the carefully groomed boy in the lace-collared blouse taken for Sunday strolls. Struwwelpeter, Dirty Peter, with his bushy forest of hair and his long fingernails, with his pals, for me stood for all my own weaknesses, fears and longings. The naïve, strong-colored pictures were like the scenery of my own dream. There were the cut-off bleeding thumbs and the big gaping shears ready to cut off more if they could, and there was Suppenkasper, the boy who just wouldn't eat when he was told, with his strict, gaunt father and his plump mother, and his words, I won't eat my supper, no, I won't, were my own words, and it was myself who rocked back and forth on the chair and who, when he fell, dragged down with him the tablecloth with all the plates and dishes full of food. That was my revenge. That was what they got for all their scolding and admonishments. And then the idealization of dying. Starving was my retaliation, with this starvation I punished them, the lean man, the fat woman, sweet was the vengeance in which I myself was devoured. To see all this in pictures relieved me, part of the inward pressure had been conjured into externals. And others too could fly through the air, just look at the boy under the umbrella. My childhood is

etched in the glossy clarity of this picture, high in the air
the flying boy with the little red umbrella, blown along
over the trees and the green field and the white church,
and behind him the black cloud with the slantwise
bursting squall of rain. Struwwelpeter and then the
wicked, sad fairy tales, these were part and parcel of the
world in which I grew up, in them was expressed a distressing, suffocating truth. These clearly displayed terrors and cruelties were better than uncertainty. It was
better to stand quite close in front of the danger and
look it in the eyes, it was better to see that it was really
there than to lie painfully in the dark and only to guess
at it. My feeling of abandonment also decreased as I saw
that others too were subjected to similar experiences, so
that I was no longer quite so lost, I belonged to a community of the bewitched, for whom everything was
strange and phantomlike. I belonged to a group of wan-
derers who had gone into the land of horror. The gruesome was my special province. Protectedness and snug
peacefulness repelled me, I felt downcast when I heard
about lovely children, kind parents, rich rewards. De-
pictions of protectedness, of warmth and content evoked
in me a searching pain. Perhaps somewhere this security did exist, these rooms that smelled of freshly baked
pretzels and in which a friendly old grandmother sat in
the rocking chair and a cat played with the ball of wool,
but for me it was old Aunty Lenelies, out there in the
wavy, headily scented fields, the spooky Corn Witch
who suddenly ran out to the edge of the path and kid-
napped the child, for me there was losing my way in the

forest, the morass with the will-o'-the-wisps and the witches' cabins. I knew what it felt like to crouch in a cage and to hold out through the bars to the witch a bone instead of a finger. I knew the fearful suspense when, right in front of me, she felt out the bone, when I heard her bleating that she wanted pretty, fat little children, nice juicy morsels, to slaughter. The parkland around our house assimilated all the fairy tales, it was enchanted, and amid its mosses, its thick bushy places, its gnarly roots like cartilage, lived animals that talked, gnomes, robbers, and fairies. Here I saw the red-bearded dwarf Rumpelstiltskin dancing, saw how he split himself in two, and here in a tumbledown farmyard at the edge of the wood, the head of the horse Falada was nailed to the wall and I heard a hollow voice within him call out, If your mother knew, if your mother knew, her heart would break. In one of these books there was a picture of two children, a boy and a girl, sitting high up in the branches of a large tree. They had lost their way in the forest and had climbed up the tree to keep a lookout. But all around there was nothing to see but green impenetrability and so they had fallen asleep, snuggled up next to each other. The picture expressed that there was no longer a way back, the lostness of the two children was so absolute that all their fear somehow vanished. Their clothes were ragged from their long wanderings, their faces showed signs of their privations, but now they were completely given up to sleep, completely shut off from the world. In this picture I found something that lay beyond witches, ghosts and monsters, complete

stillness, quiet and solitude, comfort and strength. I remember another book, with bendy, gray-green covers, a
child's Bible with illustrations in the style of the Old
Masters. I see before me a picture that depicted the princess on the banks of the Nile finding the basket in which
Moses lay. The princess is clad in a veil through whose
transparence the shape of her body may be guessed, a
female slave holds a protective fan of palm branches
over her. In my sketchbook I drew a copy of the princess, originally her whole figure with her sexual features
strongly emphasized. Then just her face, a face that became ever more immense until finally the whole sheet
was filled with her dark profile and her huge, spying
eyes. Next to the first page, which reveals that I had
given much attention to the structure of the female
body, was a pair of scissors wide open in readiness to
cut, and, as if to soothe my fear of the menace, I had
painted a jumping jack head between the gaping blades
of the scissors and on the sprawled-out puppet legs put
long boots. It was as if my own knowledge was frightening me, and then the princess's face began to look like
my mother's, the domineering dark eye, that was my
mother's eye, the eye that missed nothing. On another
page of the Bible was depicted the building of a pyra-
mid. Amid whiplashings by the guards the slaves lugged
massive stones up the sloping ramps, here and there one
broke down and perished in the dust. My fantasy was
nourished by this picture's emanations, I lived among
guards whose thongs lashed me to pieces, I savored all
the sorrows of humiliation and later, when I found *Ben*

Hur, I experienced as a chained galley slave the pleasures of direst distress. There was the captive warrior,
who, bound naked to the back of a stag, was driven into
the thorn thicket. There were the gladiators who wrestled with lions in the arena, there was the Foreign Le-
gionary who lay wounded in desert sand, beset by
prowling hyenas. The pictures that I found in the Bible,
all these pictures of persecutions and tortures, of plun-
derings and murders, of slanders and penances, all these
formed the groundwork for new visions which blended
with my destructive games. I read of steel warships
blown to pieces by grenades, of torpedoes launched
from a U-boat in which the crew listened with bated
breath as it steered toward the enemy ship's side, leaving
behind it a telltale trail of foam on the water's surface, I
read of the bloody bodies of the wounded, of comrades
rescuing each other from the flames, of heroic captains
who stuck to their posts on the bridges of their sinking
ships and allowed themselves to be sucked down with
the wreck into the depths of the ocean, I read of adventurous pirateering expeditions that landed on distant
shores, I read of fights in snowstorms on high and rocky
mountain peaks, of troops who charged out of their
trenches at night in downpours of rain, to butcher each
other in close combat in the mud, I saw the picture of
the Lancers who rode out in the pallidly luminous dawn,
and in brief doubt I asked myself where these Lancers
were riding to, and why, as the song said, they rode to an
early death, and I foresaw their folly, I felt something of
the intangible horror that was the purpose of all my

reading, when I saw the picture of the Indian prisoners brought to execution bound to the mouths of cannons and read the caption underneath that said that with such a death not only the body but also the soul is destroyed. There are scenes in a book of which I hardly know the title or author, scenes that are as unforgettable to me as scenes from *The Red and the Black*, *Hunger*, *Pan*, and *The Idiot*. There is a river in a jungle and from one bough that stretches far out over the river hangs an Indian, ready to throw himself onto the approaching canoe, a moment of extreme suspense. There is a room in a house in a provincial town, I do not know what happened in this room, nor who is in this room, there is only this room with a cupboard, a bed, and closed shutters, perhaps it is Sunday and everyone in the house is sleeping, and someone is eavesdropping here in this muffled room and is planning something and is full of expectation. There is the island on which the shipwrecked of the Pacific have landed, their reed huts rise, clearly outlined between the tall, slender palm trunks. My thought of flight to far-off lands was concentrated in this picture. The curious thing was that, considering the out-of-the-way places and sights, something like recognition arose in me, nothing was so surprising and exotic that it did not find an understanding echo somewhere within me. My reading was not selective. I was attracted or repelled according to hidden laws. Countless books I merely skimmed through, I had scarcely thumbed through their pages before I knew that they were nothing for me, many that were later to be of value to me

passed meaningless through my hand. Others capti-
vated me with a single word. *The Possessed, The Insulted
and Injured, The House of the Dead, The Devil's Elixir,
Black Flags, Inferno*—these were the titles that suddenly
flared up in front of me and lit up something within me.
There was something magical about these titles, they
went straight to my heart. Reading them, the fumbling
and searching that I had experienced in front of the
door with the red and blue panes and upstairs in the loft
matured. My whole life was a fumbling and searching. I
penetrated into music, into the architecture of fugues,
into the tortuous labyrinths of symphonies, into the
hard structure of jazz, into Oriental chimes, nothing
was unfamiliar to me. I understood the wailing of Chinese flutes and the solemnity of medieval songs, I was
filled to bursting with music, when I moved it was as if a
veil of sound jingled within me, my steps evoked throbbing drumbeats, interior instruments played continu-
ously. At home I lived like someone besieged. My room
was like a fortress. I had filled its walls with pictures of
masks and demons, and with my own drawings whose
shrieking figures frightened off the intruder. I felt the
explosive force within me and knew that I had to devote
my life to the expression of this explosive force, but at
home my attempts were regarded as aberrations of
which one did not have to take serious account. Driven
by imperious inner urge I left my room at night, naked
and in nameless excitement. I heard the mattresses
creaking under my parents' bodies, heard their heavy
breathing, perhaps they were lying sleeplessly, thinking

of my misery. I, however, crept naked into the room where my sister Margit lay. She saw me come in, sat up in bed, a street lamp projected the broken image of the window and the filigree work of the pattern on the curtains, across the wall and ceiling. Noiselessly I came to Margit's bed, sat next to her, and noiselessly we explored each other with bated breath, and Margit too stripped off her nightdress and my hands glided over the small swellings of her breasts, passed over her soft but slowly hardening nipples, spread over her belly and the childlike smoothness of her genitals, and then we lay side by side, pressed ourselves close to one another and my penis stiffened and pressed itself against the warm part between her thighs, and so we lay, mouth to mouth, while our parents in their bedroom breathed and groaned. On other evenings, when our parents had gone out, I approached Elfriede, who had been hired by our parents to take care of us. In my room we practiced something we called gymnastic exercises. Gymnastics is useful and strengthens the muscles, gymnastics refreshes the mind, no one can object to it if we place ourselves side by side and bend backward and forward or if we lean back to back with our arms linked and hoist each other into the air. That is sport. That I only wore a towel about my hips was to allow the body to breathe more freely. And Elfriede took off her dress only in order that it should not get rumpled in the course of our exertions. If we placed our hands on each other's belly or thigh, this was only for support, and if Elfriede stripped off her slip and rolled down her stockings she

did so only for the sake of greater freedom of movement. She was still decently dressed, in brassiere and
panties. Kissing was out of the question, I was not allowed to touch her breasts, though she felt my chest to
test the beating of my heart. Once when I was bending
over backward my loincloth came loose and Elfriede
rushed out with a shriek, I ran after her through the
dark corridor, the towel hanging over the stiff-out phal-
lus, followed her into her room, which was situated next
to the hall leading to the door of the flat, but just as I had
leaped over the threshold of her room, I heard the sound
of a key being turned in the door and I turned about,
fled back through the corridor, back into my room,
slipped on a dressing gown, then on a sudden inspira-
tion charged into the sitting room, switched on the radio and was sitting there, subduing my panting with
difficulty, when my mother entered in a rustling evening
gown and in glittering jewelry. It seemed to me that my
flight must still be visible in the hall outside, the imprint
of one single great leap transfixed in timelessness. This
period of my existence, full of bottled-up disaster, seems
to lie endlessly far back, further back than the earliest
days of childhood. I look at that time as if from another
life, a stranger before the I from which I have emerged.
I see the endless columns, hear the monotonous march
beat, the clatter of nailed boots, the jingling of daggers
on their belts. Again and again came the flags and the
standards, the extinguished anonymous faces, the
mouths opened in song, again and again came the
drums, and above the city a vast fire seemed to glower.

Ceaselessly the march beat throbbed, like a pulse in the city's intestines, something was being charged and gained ground, seized me, seized all of us, a force that had throbbed for as long as I could remember, and even earlier, at the time of my birth and of the mythical years when the bombardments lay dully muffled along the horizons, when the wounded bled to death in field hospitals. I too was trapped in a merciless development, and even if I was one of those who fled, I too was melted down into this ceaseless marching, it was as if I had stood here from the beginning at the curb and had seen the mass pass by, linked together and grim, my brothers were with them, armed with knotty sticks, with a look of entrancement on their faces, with steel helmets and the emblems of a new and terrible crusade. Even if, in secret, I sought after other truths, the compulsiveness of a feeling of solidarity with this marching got hold of me, the compulsiveness of the crazy idea of a common destiny. The voices of dream were suppressed by the shouted commands of reality. My anxious protests, my tiny attempts at rebellion were nipped in the bud. I could not recognize my position. Recognition only comes later when it's all over. Later I could understand and assess, but at the time I was blindly drawn along by the current. At that time I thought only of my poetry, my painting, my music. Had I not suddenly been faced with a drastic change I would have been borne along in the torrent of marching columns, into my destruction. This sudden change took place after hearing one of the speeches which in those days spewed out of the loudspeakers and which before my realization possessed an inconceivable power over me, but which afterward seemed like an incoherent screaming from hell. Next to me sat Gottfried, my half brother, and we listened to the hoarse screaming, we were overcome by this screaming, felt only that we were overpowered, we did not grasp its content, indeed there was no content, only emptiness of unprecedented dimension, emptiness filled with screaming. So overpowering was this emptiness that we completely lost ourselves in it, it was as if we were hearing God speaking in oracles. And when the hurricane of jubilant summons to death and self-sacrifice, which at the time seemed like so much cheering for a gold-gleaming future, had run its course, Gottfried said, What a pity you can't be with us. I felt neither surprise nor fear at these words. And when Gottfried then explained that my father was a Jew, this came to me like the confirmation of something I had long suspected. Disclaimed awareness came to life in me, I began to understand my past, I thought of the gang of persecutors who had jeered at me in the streets and had thrown stones in instinctive obedience to a tradition of persecution of those who were different and had inherited contempt for certain facial features and essential characteristics. I thought of Friederle, who was one day to become a model of the heroic defender of the Fatherland, and at once I was entirely on the side of the underdog and the outcast, though I still did not understand that this was my salvation. I still only grasped my lostness, my uprootedness, I was still far from taking my fate into my own hands, and making the fact of my not belonging a source of power for a new independence. Before we left the country and began our journeyings across many frontiers Margit died. On the day her dying began our house was like a greenhouse in the muggy heat before a thunderstorm. My brothers and sisters squabbled and fought among themselves, my mother, tormented by headaches, lay on her bed in the darkened bedroom and shouted for quiet. Entangled in each other like a pack of foxes my sisters and my younger brother rolled into the corridor and my mother stormed out of her room with a tennis racket in her raised hand, her face crimson and her disheveled hair streaming. The combatants scattered, I heard their footsteps fleeing along the stifling corridor and heard Margit calling, Mama's got cramps, Mama's got cramps. Those were the last words I ever heard her speak. The door of the flat was wrenched open, the footsteps died away in the echoing well of the staircase and all was quiet again. After a while I too went outside. My sisters had disappeared, my brother was gliding slowly up and down the white-hot avenue on his roller skates. In glum boredom I slouched through the streets and arrived back later in front of our house, leaned against the porch underneath our balcony, drummed out a rumba rhythm on the rough crumbling surface of the masonry and hummed la cucaracha, la cucaracha. Suddenly I heard my name being called, a soundless cry, yet I had heard it, not so much a cry as an atmospheric disturbance, a breath of cold, and I looked up to the balustrade of the balcony where Irene was leaning out, her face white and her mouth strangely twisted as if laughing, on the yellow wall between us. Then I heard Irene whispering, Margit has been run over. I rushed into the house, the door of our flat was wide open, I saw my mother standing in the depths of the hall. Ceaselessly she rubbed her hand across her face, which seemed to have gone to pieces, and without pause from her mouth came a stammering, everything's all blood, everything's all blood, everything's all blood. Lined up before her in the hallway stood my younger brother, Elfriede, and Irene, turned to stone while in flight, like playing statues, Irene still half flying, just back from the balcony, Elfriede canted sideways and looking up at me, my brother crouched down, staring up at my mother. And all the time my mother was brushing her hand across her face and her eyes were shut and her lips murmured, Everything's all blood, all blood, all blood. From out of her numbness Elfriede whispered to me that Margit was in the hospital and that they were waiting for my father to arrive. From outdoors came the sound of a car braking to a stop, right afterward my father's hurrying steps on the stairs, he ran past us, leaning forward with his coat flapping, put his arm around my mother, supported her and propelled her at his side out onto the landing. Her face was unrecognizable. We held our breath as they went out. That evening my two elder brothers came and we went together to the hospital, I walking between them. Silently we walked through the dusk, saturated with exhaust fumes, and showers of coldness ran over me. In silence we crossed the broad tree-planted forecourt of the hospital and up in the tall red façade nurses were leaning out of windows and shaking blankets and beating mattresses. In silence we approached Margit's bed and the shuddering coldness gave way to a trembling that ran right through me. My sister's head was tightly swathed in bandages, plaster concealed her cheeks and her squashed nose was stretched in a wire frame. Her grazed hands opened and contracted. A groan escaped her mouth but it sounded as if muffled by a gag. She's unconscious, whispered a nurse in a wide black robe. Her words were meant to console us but what comfort was there in the face of the frightful convulsion which suddenly brought Margit's body rearing up into a high arc, what was the use of such consolation when I could see my sister arching upward resting only on her head and toes as if stretching out in an ecstasy of voluptuousness to receive a lover, constructing a bridge between life and death. The blankets slid off her and I saw the bright smooth belly that I had felt against my body, I saw the tiny breasts I had caressed, I saw the soft curve of her womb which I had pressed with my body. The trembling came upon me, next day as I stood before the easel in my room and painted my first large picture. Three figures in white costumes, doctors or judges, loomed up out of the black background, their faces were bowed in an oppressive severity, their lowered glances refused all mercy. I painted on the following day also, still shaking with cold, and when Gottfried came into my room I had just finished the final strokes. In silence Gottfried looked at me and I knew that it was at an end. We went through the warm, dark streets. In the sickroom my parents were sitting hand in hand at the death bed. In the background the Catholic nurse moved about like a large black bird. A candle was burning on the bedside table. Trembling, I stood in front of the immovable, the extinguished. I felt as if I were floating a few inches above the floor. The bandages and the wire frame had been removed from the grazed face. It was a yellowed, squashed, completely strange face. The eyes had sunk deep into their hollows. The dead hands were folded over her chest, they were like the tapering, carved hands of a Gothic sculpture. A black crucifix, huge and incongruous, lay beneath the stiffened fingers. My parents too were like statues submerged in the half dark. My mother lay back completely exhausted in the open car as we slowly drove home. Home. There was no home any longer. The journey into the unknown had begun. Like survivors of a shipwreck in a boat we drove through the gently surging ocean of the city. Next morning I saw Margit once again. She was laid out on a slab in the hospital mortuary. Her eye sockets were covered with cotton batting. Her neatly brushed hair had lost its sheen. A fly crawled over her brow. I shooed the fly away and in doing so brushed against Margit's hair. My hand jerked back, her hair was so cold. I had never imagined that hair could be so cold. In the days that followed when the windows of our flat were draped and the curtains lifted like dark sails in the slightest breeze one could hear only now and then a whispering and a tapping of footsteps on tiptoe on the landing. My mother sat motionless in a chair, with

limply drooping arms like a clay figure. Once the pastor
came. My father carried on an almost inaudible discus-
sion with him about the memorial sermon that the unknown pastor was to read over the finished life of
someone he had not known. My brothers, my sister, and
I, the survivors, stood around the room and did not dare
to look at each other, I noticed how Irene's face sometimes sought mine, but I avoided her glance for I knew
that I would have to laugh if our eyes had met. The pastor and my father sat in the deep armchairs, the pastor
leaned over toward my father, my father's voice murmured, the pastor jotted down a few notes, wanted him
to name some typical quality, a phrase that would sum
up the essence of Margit's being, and I caught the word
sunshine. She was a ray of sunshine to us all, the pastor
said, and he tried out the sentence on his tongue. My
father nodded dumbly. Gottfried had taken charge of
negotiating with the undertakers. The coffin, the tomb-
stone, the flowers had been chosen, the musical pro-
gram to accompany the ceremony had been decided. I
followed Gottfried to the funeral parlor. Margit's body
was already hidden in the coffin and the top screwed
down over her. The coffin was lifted into the hearse, the
hearse drove off to the graveyard with Margit shut into
her coffin and with Gottfried and myself sitting next to
the driver. Through the glass window of the hearse behind me I could see the white coffin laden with wreaths
and bunches of flowers. The vibrations of the moving
vehicle made the coffin shake, and inside the coffin
my dead sister's body shook in concert. At the funeral

service we sat packed closely together in the narrow chapel pews. When the pastor's voice had died away and the sound of the word sunshine thrust into me like a knife for the last time, and when the last prayer had evaporated into the rotting scent of the flowers and wreaths and we had all dazedly worked our way out of the pews, my mother got stuck between the hassock and the armrest. My father and Gottfried rushed to her rescue and pulled her out sideways. Outside spots of sunlight were dancing. With strong bending and stretching out of arms, with arched backs and muscle-play beneath jackets, with their tensed thighs thrust forward the black-coated men lowered the white coffin down on ropes into the black hole in the earth. The pastor filled a shovel with sand, it was a little green shovel like the one we had to play with in the sandpit. My mother stood hidden behind a thick black veil supported by my father and Gottfried. From the ranks of the mourners a girl of Margit's age stepped forward, shook my mother's hand, curtsied to her and withdrew into the background, whereupon a second girl stepped forward, shook my mother's hand, curtsied to her and withdrew into the background, whereupon a third girl stepped forward, shook my mother's hand, curtsied and withdrew, whereupon a fourth girl stepped forward, shook my mother's hand, curtsied and withdrew, whereupon a fifth and a sixth girl and more girls and even more girls stepped forward, shook my mother's hand, curtsied before her and withdrew, until all the girls from Margit's class had come forward, shaken hands with my mother, curtsied

to her and returned again to their places. On the way
back we sat squashed together in one car. I crouched on
the floor, Irene half lay over me, my younger brother
almost disappeared between my father and my mother,
my father's knees dug into my chest and Gottfried's
knees were thrust into my back. My face was streaming
with sweat. Outside the summery streets flew past and
there someone stood in the dust, looking after us. This
was the beginning of the break-up of our family. Soon
this trip in which once again we clung together was at an
end, soon my stepbrothers got out and left us, soon the
city lay behind us, and after that the country in which I
had grown up, and a new life in a foreign country began.
For many years still the outward structure of the family
was to be kept intact in the carefully preserved home.
Among silver-green willow trees of an English landscape, home was set up in a red brick house; in the
mean-natured narrowness of a Bohemian industrial
city, home was set up in a dirty, yellow-colored villa; the
last time home was set up, it was in a large, dark brown
wooden house on the shores of a Swedish lake, and there
the decline that had begun with my sister's death reached
its conclusion. Our home was kept going by my parents
but even their dying had begun, even their dying had
begun with my sister's death. My sister's death was the
beginning of my attempts to free myself from my past.
There were periods when I raged and stormed about,
the suppressed revolt flared up and cursed the old forces
that had dominated me and lashed out, but the blows
fell wide of their aim and the insults reached no one's

ears. Hatred and violence were no longer of any use, the opportunities had been missed, the enemies were no longer tangible. I did not know where the enemy was concealed. I did not know what had happened to me. I was furious with myself for only in myself were there unprotected flanks to attack, only in myself was the past contained and I was the custodian of the past. Past events rose up in me like a gasping for breath, like the pressure of a straitjacket, the past would hem me around in a slow, black seepage of hours, and then suddenly recede and become nothing and allow a brief glimpse of freedom. Then I saw my parents and was full of sympathy and compassion. They had given us all that they had to give, they had given us food and clothing and a civilized home, they had given us their security and their orderliness and they could not understand why we did not thank them for it. They could never understand why we drifted away from them. In the confused knowledge of having made mistakes they bought themselves off with expensive presents, birthdays and bank holidays were the days fixed for paying out their unconscious guilt. And the presents were always wrong, however much we received we always stood there with dissatisfied faces asking for more. We never got what we wanted to have and we did not know what we wanted to have. Thus we confronted each other, children dissatisfied, parents insulted. And we were unable to explain ourselves to each other. And this obstacle I took over into myself. I took over my parents' misunderstanding. My parents' embarrassment became my embarrassment.

Their voices live on in me. I chastised and beat myself
and drove myself to forced labor. Again and again the
swamp fever of inadequacy gripped me. There I was
again, a failure at school, sitting locked into my room,
and the warm seething life outside was unattainable.
There sat my mother next to me and heard me repeat
my lessons and I could get nothing right. Schwein is pig,
pig comes from to pick—pick, pick, pick, and she took
hold of me by the scruff of the neck and pressed my nose
into the vocabulary book, pick, pick, pick, so now perhaps you'll remember it. I remembered it. At times I
could be startled out of my dream, still feeling the grip
of my mother's hand on my neck, still feel the slap of my
mother's hand on my cheek, and hear her furious voice,
see her index finger next to me travel down the keys of
the piano, to point out to me the correct note, the note
that I was unable to find, and she did not find it either,
her finger missed its mark, the dissonance still shrills in
my ears. And I take my mother's hands and put them
aside and my hand strokes her hands and I see my
mother sitting under the floor lamp, her hands busy
with pieces of clothing, her hands active, a whole lifetime at our torn stockings, shirts, and trousers, her
hands, devoted a whole lifetime to caring for us, her
hands a whole lifetime holding us, cleaning us, disci-
plining us, and suddenly these hands lie down tired,
suddenly they have served their time, and her face, lit up
by the floor lamp, stared in front of her, and her mouth
opened and the hard lines of her face relaxed, and the
face listened for the incomprehensible, and the face's

listening is so intense that it takes on a look of nameless astonishment. This had always been a part of her, the fear of being stricken dumb, of becoming paralyzed, a fear that she resisted with all her energy, and which made her domineering and angry, and which at times overcame her with sudden fainting attacks. As if struck by a terrible blow she would sink to the ground, where she then lay, a ghastly sight, like a mountain, and as she aged these states came slowly and stiflingly, lay across her chest, encased her joints with lead, deadened the power of her voice. In her diary I found the following entry, Had a dreadful dream. Mamma took me by the hand and proudly introduced me to all the people in a large room. Then we came into a hall, where on a raised dais a bluish-red eagle sat. Everyone shut into the room was led up to it and the eagle slowly forced its talons into his mouth and ripped out his tongue. I too was led there. I woke with a loud scream. My mother once said to me, you've always been a stranger to me, I'll never be able to understand you. To hear this was harder than to suffer her blows. The need to be embraced by her was not yet dead. There was one event that revealed the nervous tension in our relationship. After the period we had spent in the house in the park, we had moved to a new house. Friends of my parents had decided to celebrate our moving by a surprise party and on the evening for which this was arranged, my mother, who knew nothing of the preparation, was invited to the house of other people in the know. In ghostly haste the friends took over the house, and while they covered themselves in white sheets, bowls of various foods were produced and servants laid the table and when everything was ready someone called my mother on the phone and informed her in a dark, mysteriously disguised voice that I, who had lain that evening feverish in bed, needed her help. My mother told me later she had believed at that moment that in a feverish fit I had leaped out of the window. A terrifyingly altered reality presented itself to her as she burst into our house and through the wide opened door of the dining room saw a party gathered by candlelight around the table, all deathly still and hidden under their tall peaked hoods, and in the hall Augusta was standing and grinning and gesticulating with her arms as if she were out of her wits and my mother pushed her aside and leaped with a yell into my room, ran to the open window, leaned far out and shouted my name. Here I am, I called and sat up in bed. She spun around and, putting her arms around me, broke down before me weeping. But the heart of our relationship was touched on much earlier on our short, extraordinary journey. The doctor had advised my mother, because of my frequent illnesses, to take me to a convalescent home on an island in the sea. There I stand in this Home, a broad, smooth parquet floor stretches out in front of me, my mother has left me alone, my mother has cast me out, and my life is finished. I run over the mirrorlike smoothness of the parquet floor and land upon a path, it is a path of white sand, and in the white sand black patches occur, and the black patches become ever closer and tears stream down onto me, and I run along down

the path to the beach, and in front of me lies the vast
gray-green body of the sea and the body breathes with
rushing noises and lifts itself toward me and calls to me,
and I run to this body and I want to go into this body,
and then arms enfold me and hold me back and my
mother holds me and leads me back, but not back into
the Home, not back into exile, she elopes with me to her
room in the hotel, and in this room we sit by night, my
mother in a wicker chair beneath the window, I at her
feet, and at dawn our ship is to leave and I am alone with
my mother, have her entirely to myself, and she has
given me bank notes to play with, bank notes whose
figures promise vast riches, bank notes that will be de-
valued by tomorrow, and the bank notes rustle in my
hands and the searchlight of a lighthouse flits at regular
intervals through the room and illuminates a white
chest of drawers, a mirror, and the large flowers of the
carpet. And then the coach brought us to the landing-
stage and in the coach a man sat opposite us with a
broad black slouch hat, and his face lay in deep shadows.
On board ship, I stood on the companionway near the
bows and my senses were wide open, and I sang into the
fierce wind, and salty foam sprayed over my face and
dark snatches of cloud raced adventurously across the
lightening sky. Even if I knew nothing about my mother,
her body was tangibly there, in forceful encounters. I
had become aware of her presence, in the sounds of her
voice, in the sweaty exhalations of her sex. But my father
was unapproachable and withdrawn. In the mornings
when I washed myself next to him in the bathroom I

watched him with a searching excitement. Thin, color-
less hair spread around his large flat nipples and the
middle of his chest. His skin had a white sponginess
about it. Below the navel the beginning of a scar was visible. His genitals remained hidden, he had never been
naked in my presence. When I washed I took off my
nightshirt and bound it around my hips by the sleeves,
so that the shirt hung down over my legs like an apron.
My father surveyed my washing. Whenever he saw that
I shrank from the cold water, he would seize the wash-
cloth and rub down my face and neck with it. My father's relationship to me at home was forced. At my
mother's insistence he made himself at times a disciplin-
ing authority, which was out of keeping with his retiring
nature. When he came home after work, it sometimes
happened that my mother worked him up with a report
of my misdoings. What these misdoings really were
usually remained uncertain—perhaps it was an attack I
had made on my younger brother or sister, or a repri-
mand I had had from a teacher. In the case of exception-
ally grievous offenses, my mother waited for my father
at the garden gate, I could see her there from the room
in which I had been locked for punishment. She paced
uneasily up and down and when my father appeared
rushed toward him. I pressed my face to the pane and
followed their violent gestures with my eyes. The suspense in the pit of my stomach was like a tickle to make
one laugh. My parents came along the garden path toward the house, then my father's steps approached on
the stairs. I remained glued to the window and listened

to the manipulations of the door handle and key. My waiting for the punishment to begin was extended by the difficulties my father had to overcome to unlock the door. While he fumbled away at the door he shouted threatening words to me in order to work himself up into a fury. Finally he came rushing into the room, ran up to me, took hold of me, and bent me over his knee. As he was not strong, his blows did not hurt. But the humiliating communion in which we found ourselves was painful to the point of nausea. He beating me, I moaning, we lay over one another in a terrible embrace. I shouted for forgiveness and he shouted disconnected words, and he no more knew why he was beating me than I knew why I was being beaten, it was a ritual process forced upon us by unknown higher powers. Breathless and covered in perspiration, my father sat there, having spent his strength, and now he had to be consoled and nursed, he had done his duty, now came the reconciliation, now came the artificial family peace, my mother ran to join us, and like a single block we lay entwined in one another, sobbing tears of relief. Together we now went down into the house we inhabited together and we ate cakes and drank chocolate with whipped cream. Only on Sundays, on which I sometimes accompanied my father to his office, did the beginnings of opportunities occur for some other sort of being together. These beginnings were never allowed to develop. In the entrance hall, right next to the stairs that led up to the office, was a peepshow whose vaulted entrance was surmounted by the mask of a boy's face with empty

eye-hollows and half-open downcast mouth. In passing
I glanced anxiously up to the white visage that had wept
all its tears and had turned to stone over its pain. The
office smelled of tobacco and cold ashes, and on the
smoke-stained paneling of the wall hung framed pictures of factories and chubby, bewhiskered faces, and a
map of the world with shipping routes marked on the
blue of the oceans. Three deep leather armchairs surrounded the smoking table, on the round hammered
brass top of which stood blackly mottled ash trays and a
white porcelain elephant and wooden cigar boxes which
when their lids were raised revealed on the inside color-
ful pictures of sailing ships, dark-skinned women, an-
chors, crossed flags, and golden coins. The tall brown
bookshelves were filled with rows of files and pattern
catalogues. My father sat at his desk in front of the catalogues and opened his mail with an ivory paper knife. I
sat opposite him and in a bowl of water loosened the
stamps from letters and spread them out to dry on a
large piece of green blotting paper. Surreptitiously I
watched my father as he sat with his letters, with a grave
expression on his face, making his notes and holding in
his pale, well-manicured hands with their bluish veins
standing out a cigarette whose smoke spiraled upward.
The silence was broken only now and then by my father
clearing his throat and perhaps he looked up once and
met my gaze and smiled at me and from time to time
there was a feeble humming in the yard below where
underneath the peepshow cupola of glass protected by
wire netting a picture-drum jerkily rotated. Sometimes

I went down into the theater, the proprietress of which sat in corner darkness in a rocking chair, a toy-size dog asthmatically snoring in her lap. Usually I was the only visitor, and the proprietress let me attend several showings, I sat on a chair in front of the big black drum and pressed my eyes against the greasy glass behind which stereoscopic scenes appeared in glaringly lit stiffness. There were herds of buffalo, fleeing a prairie fire, huntsmen under the northern lights of a polar landscape being attacked by polar bears, condemned men bound fast to the block, the executioner holding the ax in readiness to let it fall, a city vanishing in an earthquake, a moon rocket just landed on a distant planet. With smarting eyes and benumbed by a feeling of dizziness, I stared at the panoramas as they hove into view, paused briefly, and then turned on again. Most impressive was the room in which the thief crouched in front of the bureau drawer he had just broken open. It was a refined, well-cared-for room. The cushions on the sofa were squashed down as if someone had just sat in them, a book lay open on the table under the lamplight, and the fire was burning in the grate, the only disturbing thing was the dog, who lay with legs outstretched on the floor. The thief's hands were sunk deep in the drawer, and his face, concealed up to the eyes by a black cloth, was peering toward the open door, as if he had heard some sound in the darkened hall outside. And now I am in London, standing in the storerooms of my father's office, between the samples table and shelves filled with rolls of cloth, and a rankling uneasiness wells up in me, I lean forward

and hold my breath and look through the glass window
of the door into the office where my father, slim and
erect, sits at his desk and his partner, spongy and flabby,
leans on the table next to him and bends over it. The
partner's clucking voice jabs insistently at my father,
who glances up at him with his head on one side. At the
back of the room, a Miss Gray sits and hits the typewriter keys with her fingers. I sit down at the samples
table, press myself close to the edge and pull a book out
of my pocket. I set the book down in front of me at the
edge of the table under the cover of a voluminous store-
room catalogue. I open the book and begin to read while
a tiny guard on my shoulders is watching and keeps an
eye on the door and while my hand lies on the alert with
raised pencil in the lists of the catalogue. The words of
the book penetrate into me, while I feel the stone floor
on the soles of my feet, while above the thick glass
squares set into the ceiling, a ceiling covered with map-
like stains, there was a rolling of cartwheels and a darkness of shoe clickings, while in the outer office there was
whispering and stirring, while unease radiated from my
stomach into chest and bowels. "It was during the time I
wandered about and starved in Christiania: Christiania,
this singular city, from which no man departs without
carrying away the traces of his sojourn there." Then the
guard clapped me on the shoulder, his other small, hard,
flat hand at my throat, the door opened, and the warehouse clerk entered with wheezing breath and heavy,
creaking tread. Disheveled gray hair fluttered about his
head, the bristles of his beard shone silver. I slid the

book down onto my lap and back into my pocket. The
warehouse clerk sat down opposite me at the other end
of the long table. Between us ran the thick lines of the
grain of the table-top, cut across here and there by knife
marks. The warehouse clerk dug a flat green flask out of
his pocket, uncorked it, raised it to his mouth, took a
couple of gurgling swallows, wiped the back of his hand
across his lips, and thrust the flask back into his pocket.
My gaze fastened onto his emptily staring but powerful
face with its big, dirty pores. His jacket was threadbare,
his shirt greasy, his trembling stubby hands were busy
with a bundle of gray dog-eared papers. To his mouth he
lifted an indelible pencil, short and thick as if crushed
between his fingers, and moistened the tip with his
tongue, leaving a violet dot on it like a pearl. Miss Gray
appeared in the doorway and called to me. My father
wanted to speak to me. I went into the adjoining room.
My father was still sitting at his desk, he was leaning far
back in his swivel chair into the yielding back rest, while
the partner sat on the desk in front of him and bent over
him, bubbling over with talk, his sausage-like hands
folded on his stomach, his face with its fatty double chin
and bushy eyebrows rocking up and down. I stood next
to Miss Gray and smelled the dry, stale odor of her body.
She smiled nervously with her faulty teeth, and a slight
blush spread over her downy skin. I saw my face in her
pupils, my image had penetrated into her head and
stared dully back at me from her eyes. My father turned
to me, drawing away to one side from his partner's ad-
vancing bulk. The face my father turned to me was of a

sickly yellowish hue, and I saw a few beads of sweat stand out on his brow. His face was pleading, I could see that his partner had the advantage over him, he was the native here, not only a partner in the firm, he was its founder and owner and had taken my father on out of charity. My father's hand felt its way down to the handle of the leather samplecase. He said that he had to visit the manager of a department store and asked me to go along. I took the case from him and we went out into the alleyway. Dark, shaggy horses, the muscles in their haunches rippling with every step, stamped past us, their hoofs striking sparks from the cobbles, and rays of light flickered through the rotating spokes of the cart-wheels. A booming of bells tumbled down from the dome of St. Paul's. I went with my father through the surge of bells and my father described the manager of the department store to me. From his voice I could feel how he was trying to give himself courage, how he wanted to make himself and me believe that the manager was waiting for him with friendly feelings and that the visit to him was bound to be a great success. Surrounded on all sides by the clangor of the bells and the aggressive cries of the newspaper vendors, I felt how my father was trying to win me for his occupation, how he was trying to paint a rosy future for me in business. For a few paces I forgot where I was, the roaring surf of bells and the rushing of automobiles on whose hoods burned white jets of flame and the rattling and ringing of the red double-decker buses, behind whose windows huddled rows of faces, became lost in the soughing and the

brooding of my shapeless world of thought. Before we
entered the office of the department store manager, I
had crossed a sunken Vineta. We waited on an upright
wooden bench. My father had opened the leather case
and taken out a few patterns. He pointed out the quality
of material to me. His voice was uncertain and strained.
A girl with platinum blonde hair came and led us along
a corridor, as she walked her hand with its red-varnished
fingernails pressed and remolded the bun of hair on her
neck. She opened a door for us and out of the blinding
brightness of the room the manager of the store came
toward us, with elegantly cut suit and broadly jutting,
padded shoulders, gold glittering, effervescent, laughing. He patted my father with his hand as one pats a
horse, led him to a table as if to a crib, and helped him to
empty out the case of samples. My father, with delicately
testing fingers, spread out the pieces of material on the
table. The manager's hands swooped with sprinkling
gestures onto the material, rubbed and tugged at it and
flipped it over. Quipping as he picked at it with sharp
fingers he made his selection, while my father every
now and then winked at me confidentially and his pale
hands with their narrow knuckles and the evenly mani-
cured polished fingernails lay expectantly on the edge of
the table. The room was a block of light with glittering
windows. In this block of light hovered the reflecting
surfaces of the table tops. At times figures with dissolved
contours went through the room. Above the gleaming
surface with the multicolored scraps of material, my father and the store manager were coming to a business

agreement. With a friendly gesture, the store manager consented to my entering his firm as an unpaid assistant. I hardly realized what they were saying and immediately afterward forgot it, my father and the manager stood dark blue in front of me with curiously gleaming shirts. On the way back to my father's office I slipped off into side-streets. I went among old-fashioned houses and tall castle walls, crossed a courtyard with a well, and entered a workshop. Inside a spacious room, borne up by high pillars, my pictures hung on the walls. For a few moments I interrupted myself and moved between the shelves filled with bales of material and the samples table in my father's office, and compared the data on a list with the goods actually on the shelves. Then I went out in my yard, saddled a horse and rode over furrowed fields toward a rugged mountain ridge, at the border of a copse sat ragged figures armed with knives and halberds, slowly I rode past them, the bridle jingled, the typewriter clattered, the voice of the partner in the firm murmured at my father, and between the bare birch trunks shimmered large horned animals and the white torso of a woman. Toward evening I stood at the window of my room. Against the sloping gray walls leaned the few pictures I had managed to produce in my spare time. In the depths of the house lived my parents and my brother and sister. Blue dusk enveloped the garden. The striking of golf balls resounded from the links. The windowpane tasted bitter. A figure appeared from the shrubbery in green hunting clothes, with a game bag and a gun on his shoulder. With springy strides the

figure crossed the meadow and disappeared in the hedge
on the other side of the garden. A soft warm terror arose
in me. It was as if a hand had reached into myself. I sat
down at the desk on which my manuscripts lay, lit the
lamp and thumbed through the pages in which in
monkish script I informed the world of my long past
life. I had lived centuries ago, here at my desk I conjured
up pictures and words that told of my lost existence.
Steps that sounded on the stairs woke me from my oth-
erness. They were Elfriede's steps. Elfriede had moved
with us, her room was next to mine. She did not close
the door behind her. I heard her lighting a cigarette,
brushing her hair, shedding her clothes. I got up and
went on tiptoe to the door of my room. Below, my father
was locking the house up for the night. My mother's
footsteps approached. Now she was coming up the stairs
to the attic floor, the stairs creaked under the weight of
her body and she was breathing heavily. I retreated into
the middle of the room. The latch of my door was
pressed down and my mother entered. Are you still up,
she asked, what are you doing. I'm working, I said. She
glanced around the room. She saw the papers on my
desk and asked, What's that you're writing there. Nothing special, I murmured evasively. Don't stay up too
long, she said, and took the blanket off my bed. She
turned back the top sheet and smoothed the pillow, then
came toward me, took me in her arms and kissed me.
When she had left the room, I went to the door again. I
heard my mother let herself down the stairs step by step,
in slow, heavy treads. Doors were opened and doors

were shut, my mother went from room to room making
her evening rounds. Quietly I pressed down my door
latch. I went to the next door that stood ajar and pushed
it open, Elfriede sat in a short nightdress on the edge of
her bed. I slid my hands over her shoulders and hair and
she drew herself toward me, and clasped me in her arms
and her mouth sucked at my mouth. I pulled her night-
gown up above her outspread thighs. Elfriede undid my
trousers and I had trapped myself in the obligation to
perform an unintelligible task. Elfriede, breathing excit-
edly, put her hand around my penis and pulled it near
the opening between her legs. Form and content of the
task facing me were disconnected, made no sense. Elfriede, awaiting my penetration, closed her eyes, and
when she opened her eyes again I had disappeared. I
was in my room and had locked the door behind me. I
paced up and down in my room. I had taken off my
shoes so that my steps could not be heard. I imagined
myself packing my pictures together and leaving the
house. But I did not know where I could go with my
pictures. Wherever I set them up in my thoughts, someone always came and moved them on. Finally I saw myself spreading them out on the road and lying down
next to them and the tall red buses driving over us. Next
day I was in the department store. The perfect clerk always carries a pair of scissors with him, said the floor
manager, and thrust a pair of scissors in my breast
pocket. Through his pince-nez he inspected my suit and
my stiff white collar. Here everyone has to wear a stiff
collar, no one dares say No to a stiff collar. He twirled his

little waxed mustache and showed me around my new place of work. In the interior of the storage rooms the rank growth of a primeval tropical world had been turned to stone. Lianas, roots, and fern fronds twined around the pillars, the vaulting and the balustrades. The walls and ceilings of the rooms were overgrown with mushrooms, fungi, and moss. The merchandise lay piled up in stalactite caverns. Among gritty rocks, thorns, and gnawed bones lay handles and sandals, blazers and razors, chests and vests, towels and trowels, cradles and ladles, pulleys and woollies, books and hooks, prongs and tongs, pins and bins. In the subdued light of the jungle orange-yellow salesgirls fluttered around like butterflies. In the depths of a white-tiled cellar I took up my first station. Behind the narrow table that stretched the whole length of the disproportionately long room, I bent with other condemned ones over the opened sample books. The city seamstresses came down to us, carrying between the fingers of their raised hands scraps of silk and velvet, linen and damask, spiked on needles, our fingers stretched out toward them, took hold of the needles with the many-colored bits of material and wandered with them across the pages of the book, to find a piece of material that corresponded to the sample. And when a suitable item had been found, numbers, letters and names were noted down on labels, and with these the seamstresses began their journey up into the higher reaches of the building. Our faces approached each other across the table, we whispered questions in their ears under the tickling blonde, black, red, or brown hair, breathed in the skin fragrance of violet and snow-drop, drew the points of our needles scratchily over nipples that stood out from under their thin blouses. To avoid the stifling air of the cellar, we went many times a day to the washrooms, where the slamming metal doors of the clothes lockers clashed like cymbals. We sat in the toilets, whose walls were scratched full of fertility symbols and whose floors were smeared with spittle, urine and trodden butts. Here we sat, bent forward, and from the cubicles all around came a groaning and an inarticulated stammering, in a trance we sat amid the rush and drip of the plumbing, and on our shoulders we carried the burden of the vast, over-laden building. At midday we bounded up the sloping corridors to the street, past the time clock whose teeth hacked into our cards with a ping. Outside we forced our way through the solid ranks of vehicles, played toreador with the cars, beat our fists on the growling metallic beasts, hurtled into the crashing and whirling of the feeding places, gobbled down potatoes in congealed fat, beans, and pieces of stringy bacon. A tightness under the collar, a retching feeling in one's stomach. Back through the throng. Briefcases and braces, pin stripes and pipes, wheels and squeals, seams and hair creams, tires and wires, hoofs and tubes, suitings and hootings, tie pins and pink gins. In the jungle of the store I was given the task of helping the window decorator collect material for his displays. On a piece of paper he wrote me out a list of the goods he needed, and I glided and skidded to and fro between the display window that was to be decorated, and the various

departments that were to provide the necessary material. I soon lost the list, the mass of goods filled me with
hectic enthusiasm, blindly I hurtled back to the showcases and snatched up whatever came to hand. I piled
up a mountain of goods inside the display window and,
as the decorator had disappeared, I myself decorated the
display window. In the hot glass terrarium I vaunted the
surplus of the department store, surrounded myself
with matches and hatchets, sandpapers and capers, guns
and buns, ash trays and hair sprays, rubber boots and
canned fruits, nails and pails, pliers and wires, envelopes
and soaps, utensils and stencils, and I myself adopted
the pose of an entranced tailor's dummy exposing itself.
And outside, beyond the glass, the passersby applauded
me, a little sea of faces rocked and laughed, the whole
street laughed, the cars tittered, the buses held their
sides with laughter, policemen thrust themselves in between, their faces like red balloons, swollen with laughter. But hands grabbed me from behind and pulled me
up and a yellow blind banged down at the window, and
sharp eyeglasses flashed at me, and the scissors were
pulled out of my breast pocket, I had proved unworthy
of them. After this attempt I went on strike. But despite
my strike I was subject to the laws of our household.
After the grandfather clock in the hall below had struck
seven, the day began. At the bottom of the stairs my father cleared his throat and called to me. I did not reply.
He came up the stairs, opened the door of my room and
said, it's time to get up. I got out of bed and dragged my
feet down to the bathroom and washed myself next to

my father. We did not speak to one another. I dressed myself and went down to the breakfast table. My place was here at table at the family meal. My disease was still regarded as merely temporary. My father asked, Don't you want to go with me to the office. I did not reply. Without saying good-bye, wounded by my silence, my father left the table. I could not make my parents realize that for me painting and writing were work. The accusation from outside had steeped me in profound listlessness. Every day I began my work with a feeling of absolute uselessness. I painted with the colors of entrails, the colors of feces, urine, gall, pus, and blood. After a few hours I succeeded in working myself into forgetfulness. I painted until the dusk rose up from the garden and turned all the colors to black. When I had finished a picture, some urge compelled me to call my mother over. I knew how incomprehensible my pictures were to her, but I could not prevent myself from showing my pictures to her each time. I stood next to her and watched her looking at my picture. I showed her a picture of myself. I wanted her to stand a long time in front of this picture. She uttered a few non-committal words. You must move closer to it, I said, so that you can see the details. I can see it very well, she said, and turned away. I knew that I had only a short term of grace. I knew that I could not live here much longer on their charity. I lived like an obedient dog. I snapped up the scraps that I was thrown. I crept away and waited for the moment of an ultimatum. This moment came one green evening in the green garden room. My parents had called me to them.

They sat sunk in the green armchairs, my progenitors who had brought me up for seventeen years. What happened in this hour before I ran to the telephone and got myself caught up in the cord. Today I see my father and my mother after a year in a foreign country tired and lost. I see the shadows in their ailing faces, I see my mother's hands pressed into her lap as if holding back some pain, I see my father's shoulders drooping after the day's exertions. They sat here in their home that they had preserved, they sat in their green chairs in front of the tall green curtains and outside dusk settled on the green garden and their postures expressed their uprootedness, they were frightened of the future, and when they glanced at me their faces were full of concern on my account. I see myself today as they saw me then, I did not understand what unimaginable effort it had cost them to keep this home with all its inhabitants alive. You can't keep on living like this, said my father, you can't keep on being a burden to me in the situation we're in now, can't spend all your time daydreaming, the world isn't the way you think, you can never exist in it with your pictures and poems. I see myself as they saw me then, there I stood in front of them in the half dark, greenish room, I said nothing, I never said anything, just stood there tight-lipped and frozen, with my hands helplessly hanging down, perhaps I was really ill, mentally ill, and then my mother began to groan, she got up from the chair and raised her arm, made a few lurching steps toward the window, and her groaning became worse, and she sought for a grip with her hand and the hand gripped tightly into the curtain and then she crumpled at the knees, tore the curtains down with her, and fell backward onto the carpet, pressing the curtains protectively around her waist. My father jumped up and shouted to me to call the doctor, and while I was rushing to the telephone my mother groaned, No, not the doctor, not the doctor, it's just this always being upset. And I stood at the telephone, receiver in hand, the cord coiled about my arm and in the receiver buzzed the voice of the exchange and I saw a dark patch spread in the curtain, where my mother had held it pressed over her pelvic region. Just put me in bed, my mother said, then it will be all right again, don't get a doctor, I don't want a doctor, and I replaced the receiver and freed my arm from the cord. And then we dragged Mother between us to the stairs and blood dripped from her womb onto the floor, and on the narrow stairway my mother lay like a mountain between us, and my father's back rubbed along the wall and at my back the banisters creaked and bent and the grandfather clock with the sun face ticked, and behind us the shapeless shadow of the Sandman panted up the stairs. Later, when my mother had calmed down in bed, I went out into the garden, and my younger brother came to me with the small models of his racing cars. It was already almost dark in the garden and light fell on us from the kitchen, where Elfriede was preparing the evening meal. On the path that led around the meadow, we let our model cars take off in a race, and we urged on our favorites, which we had given fantastic names, with shouts of encouragement, and as the

darkness thickened it swallowed up the last of my childhood. Now every day for many months I followed my
father to the office. After office hours I often sat in a
small Russian café near Hyde Park, half a story below
street level. Here I met Jacques for the first time. I lent
him my coat when he wanted to go out into the rain
with his jacket collar turned up. He left his tattered at-
taché case as a pledge. I looked into the case and saw
that it contained a few carpenter's tools, I had rather
expected to find leaves of notepaper in it. His face was
small and finely chiseled, with a jutting chin and a sharp,
hooked nose, his hair was bushy and tousled and his
eyes, with their steely gray lustre, lay deep in their hollows. When he came back he sat down by me at the table. He informed me that he had spent the last few weeks
as a construction laborer in the country. He laughed at
my questioning glance and, pretending to hold a violin
under his chin, described fingerings with one hand and
moved the other through the air as if holding a violin
bow, at the same time whistling Bach's concerto for two
violins. I joined in with the second violin. After the concerto I told him about my pictures, which in the last few
months had been quite extinguished in me, and as I
talked about them, they came alive again and regained
their colors, and I noticed that my customary way of
talking had disappeared, that with these words I was
learning how to speak in a new way. By evoking my pictures for Jacques I was reminded that I possessed another life, a different life from my life between sample
catalogues and rolls of material, and gasped for breath. I

painted for Jacques my visions of apocalyptic landscapes
with rustling fires, fleeing animals, drowning and vanishing cities, my visions of the crucified and scourged, of
terribly distorted masks and seductive women's faces.
The pictures that arose spread out before us and took us
up into their depth, we wandered through the antique
cities and rocky wildernesses, the ruined halls and enchanted gardens. Jacques built even more into these
landscapes. Everywhere we found forms, sounds, con-
cordances. At times we were caught up in wild laughter,
it was a laughter that burst out as if a spell had been
broken. We sat next to one another at a table in a café in
a basement in a rain-sodden street in a vast city in a
strange land in the endless world and laughed so much
that tears streamed down our faces. Shaken by laughter
I talked of my existence at the office, of my existence at
home, the life I led there was so improbable that I could
only laugh about it. In my conversation with Jacques I
suddenly lost all fear of life, everything was possible to
me. Jacques had already fought himself free, he had already conquered his consuming freedom. He had exposed himself to unprotectedness and wounds. In his
life there was the wildness and unruliness that I had
sought, but also the hunger and the distress. In his presence I crept out of my cocoon and hoisted my colors and
made my thoughts scintillating and extravagant and
thus we unwound our worlds to each other and gave
each other rebuslike glimpses into our past, our dreams,
our hopes for the future. I saw scaffolding on which
Jacques balanced, I saw him playing the violin at a night

club, I saw the violin disappear into the pawnbroker's.
Jacques showed me the house where he had grown up,
the wide entrance hall through which he fled, at its side
doors of carved oak, mirrors, tinted, lead-framed windows. In his past an old, gray servant in red livery, in the
park dogs who bounded after him up to the door. The
wrought-iron latticework, the iron roses, the heavy
latch, then the country roads. Surrounded by our images we went through the city, the rain had petered out,
the sinking sun shone through the smoke, and our cata-
racts of laughter continually broke loose, everything
grew wavy, as in the mirrors of a fun house. A nimbus
of glorious perspective surrounded us, our future lay
open, I saw wide walls hung with my pictures and
Jacques directing the orchestra. In the train on our way
to the suburb where I lived with my parents we changed
the basic elements of our being into music, we were the
sounding instruments in the rhythms of the wheels and
above in my room under the sloping roof we built a
fugue with our voices from the raw material of our
hopes. From the unpatterned and as yet unspoken arose
transparent blocks of sound, grew, split up, towered one
above the other. Later this edifice dissolved in darkness,
we listened to the vanishing melodic lines, we returned
again to the realm of words and pictures, lay among the
drawings and the painted panels, among the manuscripts and books, until we no longer understood our
words and each of us sank into the shaft of sleep. Next
morning my mother stood beside me in the kitchen and
began to attack my friendship with him. I don't like the

look of him, she said, he has dangerous eyes. Next to her
on the kitchen table sat a cockroach, its front legs crossed
and rubbing each other, and looked at my mother. The
floor was covered with cockroaches, they swarmed up
the walls and disappeared, one after another, headfirst
and rowing with their back legs into the crevices. The
cat walked among them with high, disgusted steps and
bit one of the cracking bodies, drew back its mouth
from the slime that oozed out of it. My father shouted,
Hurry up, I'm going now. I answered, I'm going later
today, my friend Jacques is here, we are going to give
an exhibition of my pictures in town. What did you say,
he called, an exhibition. Yes, I replied, an exhibition,
Jacques knows someone who has an empty room where
we want to hang up the pictures. My mother stamped
her foot on the floor, the cockroach on the table started
moving, ran around in a circle several times and then
stopped at the edge, shaking its tiny head and quivering
with its feelers. My mother swept off the roach with a
brush, it fell hard and dry onto the floor and scrambled
quickly up the wall where it forced its way into a crack,
its pointed hindquarters with the crooked, bristly legs
rocked up and down for a while before it disappeared.
Upstairs in my room Jacques stood ready with my pictures. Jacques. A thirteen-days' conversation. A thirteen-
days' dream we had shared in which everything within
us that sought for expression was discussed. Far away
stood the totem poles of my father and my mother. Their
words ran off me. They stared at me full of horror as at a
condemned man. While we were lighting up layer after

layer of our inner being, with energy unpent we roamed the city. We hung my pictures up in a room over a garage in a courtyard in a concealed mews in the vast city in the strange land in the endless world. We sent out cards announcing my exhibition. No one came. We did not care. The pictures were there for us, they grew for us, they developed for us. For thirteen days every breath was fruitful, everything we touched unfolded itself and put forth blossom. Silent courtyards saw our pantomimes. Archways heard our oratorios. Dockside pubs were recipients of our thoughts' genius. But then suddenly a gray shadow fell. We felt tired. What would happen now. Now I had either to break loose entirely from the old or sink back into it. On the thirteenth day I accompanied Jacques, who had stayed overnight with us, to the station. I don't know why he wanted to go to town, perhaps some chance of a job had turned up, perhaps he was tired of me. Now this morning is quite saturated by the feeling of departure, this English summer morning with shimmering sunlight through the early mist, with the sleepy rattling of a lawn mower and the distant clatter of horses' hoofs. There lay my brother's tin pistol on the garden path, I picked it up, took it with me, Jacques spoke to me of Spain, of the Civil War, perhaps he expressed a desire to join the International Brigade. Now, looking back on this morning, it contained a final farewell, but at the time there was some agreement to meet in town, it was all over, no more to go on, I shot Jacques dead as he stood there behind the lowered carriage window. I raised the tin pistol, aimed, and imitated a shot, and Jacques pretended to be hit, threw up his arms and fell backward. The train set itself in motion and disappeared in the tunnel behind the station. Jacques did not appear again at the window, I never saw Jacques again. For a long time I looked for him. He left no trace behind. His name was not contained in the official records. I have often thought about this strange figure, and have sought to interpret it. It contained much that I should have desired, this complete license, this freedom to come and go as he liked, this vagabond's life, in my thoughts I idealized his existence, I dreamed of its extravagance and audacity as I sank back into my old imprisonment. Other things, however, made me suspicious, the impulse in him to make up lies and exaggerations, for instance, or his mystifications and his dressings up, sometimes appearing with a false beard, or with a big pair of horn-rimmed glasses, or with his wrists and forehead bandaged. His uniqueness, it seems today, lay in the very brevity of his appearance. He gave a guest performance. With prodigal intensity he built up a friendship, then when he felt it had reached its peak, he withdrew. He wanted the extraordinary. I was too slow on the ball for him, after the brief flight I lost my strength and could not follow him into his dubious and adventurous exploits and so he abandoned me, his role was at an end. Sometimes I thought, Perhaps I was mistaken, perhaps it wasn't a toy pistol I shot him with, but a real revolver, perhaps I have really killed him, and these thoughts go together with dreams that recur at intervals and in which I am involved in duels with an adversary, or an alter ego, and in which there is only one choice, you or I, and either he will murder me, coming slowly and threateningly closer, with his knife, his gun, or his terrible bare hands, or I will plunge the dagger into his body, or fire my pistol into his dissolving face. After Jacques's disappearance I returned to being a piece of furniture in the communal household, I stood at my appointed place, and when we moved to the Bohemian town in which my father was to take over the management of a textile factory I allowed myself to be shipped with them. There I lay in the evenings in the living room under the table, with the dog. I pressed the dog's head close to me, felt his warm breath on my face and clutched with my hands at his soft coat. You, Harras, I whispered, and the sheepdog laid his paws on my arm and gazed at me with his big, black eyes, and his tongue licked me. From this low vantage I saw my father sitting in the armchair glancing through the paper and my mother at the sewing table, her hand gliding up and down with the needle. On a sofa tucked away in one corner of the room sat my brother with his schoolbooks, while in another corner my sister Irene bent with her short-sighted eyes over a letter. The room was warm and clean, white curtains hung at the window, the books stood tidied on their shelves, the grandfather clock ticked in the hall. I too was thought of as part of the imposing whole. The look of the place had been settled once and for all. The piece of furniture that I was in this home was all polished and put in place and the dirt forever settling down on me forever wiped off. No one ever asked where it came from, this distressing dirt that trickled out of me, no one ever inquired, they just rubbed, brushed and polished, tirelessly, so that the shameless spot was never seen. When my mother looked down at me over the top of her spectacles pain seethed up in me and something within me urged me to crawl to her and lick her hand. I held more tightly to the dog, we belonged to one another in our dumbness. Nothing could be explained. My life was a dull waiting for the catastrophe. My father folded up his newspaper and got up. He said that it was time to go to bed. Each of us slowly worked himself out of his hole. We said goodnight to our mother. She embraced us as if we were setting off on a long journey, pressed us to her and kissed us. Oppressed and embarassed, I took leave of my father. Sometimes in my need for reconciliation I gave him my hand and got nothing but cool, dry fingertips which he hastily withdrew. I crept out of the room and my brother joined me, the dog following. We went out into the bare garden and got caught up in our games in which the lostness and instability of our existence was expressed. While we strolled over the clayey fields and woods of the neighborhood, we were changed into explorers in unknown regions of the world. We came across strange creatures and were involved in dangerous battles. We composed documents that we blackened with smoke and splashed with red paint to show that one or the other of us had been taken prisoner and was awaiting sentence of death. With the help of complex spy rings we discovered each other, liberated each other from the deepest dungeons

and out of the hands of the most gruesome inquisitors.
It seemed as if there were more reality and topicality in
these games than in my work upstairs in the loft. These
games were psychodramas in which we tried to adapt to
an emigrant existence, and in my work all was alienation and concealment. My room was in our landlady's
apartment in the top floor of the villa. To reach my room
I had to pass through her hall. The widow lived on this
floor that was filled with flower pots and smelled sourly
of cabbage. When I came through the door to the flat,
she stuck out her gray head from behind the leaves of
some plant or out of a niche and stared at me distrust-
fully from her close-set eyes. From dawn till dusk she
shuffled about, swept and clattered about in her hall, I
locked my door and hung a cloth over the keyhole. Only
at night was I free from her sniffing around my door.
Then I was alone in the rushing quietness of a vacuum,
alone with my pictures and my written pages, alone with
my books and my music. I muffled the record player
with blankets. From an immeasurable distance the music came to me, like a dream of liberation. I stood in my
grotto and my hands danced in time to the music. In my
blood and in the vibrations of my nerves, in my pulse
and my breathing sounded the music. Tears streaming
down my cheeks I drank in the music, and then went to
the spirit-voices of books, carried on imaginary conversations with the people of the books, they seekers like
myself, and to me the books were secret messages, letters in a bottle dropped out at sea to find kindred spirits.
Everywhere, in the most distant cities, on desolate

coasts, in the seclusion of woods, these individuals lived and many spoke to me from the kingdom of the dead. This concept of belonging together consoled me. It seemed to me as if the man whose book I was now reading must know of my presence, and when I sat down myself to write, I knew that others were listening for me through the great rushing noise that surrounded us all. When I saw Haller's name for the first time on the back binding of a book, a memory was awakened in me of a head gardener who appeared in a book out of my childhood. This head gardener, who had lived with his family in the jungles of South America, gave to the name of the writer Haller its first depth effect. The dedication on the flyleaf of his book roused my interest. It came from a friend of my parents, who had immigrated to China, had there been converted to Buddhism, and later committed suicide. My parents had spoken of him only in disparaging terms. He had left his family, it was hinted that he even threatened his wife with a gun. He had withdrawn from everyday life and disappeared. The words he had confided to my parents in his nervous, scratchy handwriting outflowing onto the absorbent paper were, This book is written by a brother of mine. I removed Haller's book Only for the Crazy from the orderly row on the shelf, I freed it from its unappreciative environment and let it speak out in my own realm. Reading Haller's works was like probing into my own pain. Here was a blueprint of my situation, the situation of the bourgeois who wants to become a revolutionary but is crippled by the weight of established convention.

In many ways these readings held me fast in a romantic no man's land, in self-pity and nostalgic longings, I could have used to advantage a harder and more cruel voice, one which would have torn the veil from my eyes and made me rise and shine. The "I" that I was carrying around with me was used up, destroyed, useless and had to go by the board. But how could I get to do that, how free myself from everything that was dragging me down, poisoning and stifling me. Where could I find the energy. The difficulties were bound to force me more and more into a corner. There was no other way but the way of disintegration and decay. Changes occurred with infinite slowness, one hardly noticed them. Sometimes I felt a sharp jolt and then I believed that something had become different, and then the underground waters closed in over me again and hid what I had gained in mud. Thus I felt my way along until I believed I was on the track of something new again, and one day something actually would be there, perhaps I would find firm ground beneath my feet. When I wrote to Haller it was an attempt to escape my unreality. And I received an answer to my letter. There stood my name on the envelope, I read it again and again. Suddenly I had entered into an inconceivable relation to the outside world. Someone had written my name on a letter, someone believed in my existence and directed his voice to me. I read the words of a living mouth. I was almost indifferent to the meaning of these words. The fact that someone spoke to me was enough. They were the words of an aged, humble craftsman. Perhaps I was disappointed by

the quietness and tiredness, the reserve and the suffer-
ing in this voice. Perhaps I had expected a signal for rebellion. The voice was too remote for me in its mature
wisdom. It spoke of patient work, of slow, thorough
studying, of the necessity of some means of livelihood,
and of the dangers of isolation. Only much later did I
understand Haller's words. At the time I was too impatient. The words were too mild, too conciliatory for me.
The words stood on the side of the orderly and the con-
sidered. I longed for the other extreme, the extreme of
blind self-abandonment to the extremes of the unruly
and the instinctive. I longed for it, but did not understand it, I groped in the dark and everything slipped
through my fingers. It was decided I should go to Prague
and take up an apprenticeship in a textile factory. A
room was rented for me not far from the factory. The
minute I set foot in this room I knew I would never stay.
Experimentally I filled the walls with my pictures and
drawings, spread out my papers about me, and then lay
down weakly on the sofa, while behind the pane of
frosted glass in the door the sounds and shadows of a
strange family came and went unsteadily. Next morning
I went to the factory to present myself to the Director.
The building rose like a fortress in the midst of broad,
dry fields. Inside in the workshops the looms hummed
in long rows, and the working girls were cocooned in
the close, whirring threads. In a small room I made my
mission known by shouting above the roar of the machines and men in white coats handed me on to each
other until I landed up in front of the Director, from

whose words, as far as I could tell, hindered as I was by
the foreign language and the ceaseless roar, I thought I
gathered that he had to turn me down on grounds of
competition, since my father ran a similar factory. Already he had turned away and the assistants in the white
coats, having wheeled me around, shoved me off and
away out through the screaming rows of machines. Triumphantly I walked past the cocooned weaver girls who
turned their pale faces after me, ran across the fields and
into my new freedom. What now happened had been
long since prepared, it was the moment in which after
years of pressure the bars around me fell away. I packed
my belongings together and stood with my suitcase all
on my own, out on the sidewalk. Haller had given me
the address of a man from whom I might expect advice
and help. Max B. lived in a boardinghouse near the
freight yard, his room was veiled in dense tobacco fumes
and Max lay in bed in a woolen coat with a green scarf
around his neck, half buried under newspapers. His
slabby, bony face lit up when I mentioned Harry Haller's
name. The account of my suddenly and unexpectedly
won freedom roused him out of his lethargy to which
four years of emigration had reduced him. From the
very first moment there was an understanding and trust
between us, I who was twenty years his junior, embodied the hopes and possibilities that he had long since
given up. I had a future ahead of me and immediately
Max championed this future, on the same afternoon we
looked up all his contacts who might be useful to me.
The editor of a newspaper, a dark, owlish man to whom

I showed my drawings, gave me a commission to do illustrations for him, the head of a school of graphic arts
recommended me to a professor of the art academy
who, after he had studied my work, assured me that I
would be able to enter his class. Thus on the afternoon
of the same day on which I had set off as I thought to
take up employment in a textile factory, I found myself
in the light-flooded studio of the academy and my new
comrades in their paint-smeared smocks gave me
friendly smiles. This upheaval in my life had been accomplished with effortless ease but after only a few
hours the old darkness and heaviness welled up in me
again and extinguished all the brightness. I had no right
to this freedom, I did not believe that it could have been
handed to me on a platter, I must have got it by stealth,
have sneaked into a preserve where I did not belong.
Although the professor attempted in a letter to persuade
my parents of my needing to paint, I was filled with feelings of guilt, and foreboding. In the evening in Max's
room on the sofa, which had been made up as a bed for
me, a swamp fever buzzed in me, my throat, my chest,
my head were inflamed by the bacilli of the old, unre-
solved pestilence, and then Max suddenly came to me,
naked, his tall, lean, hairy body glaringly lit up by the
lamp on the ceiling and his penis erect. He approached
me and in his approach I understood his great need for
closeness and tenderness and his helpless attempt to
break through the long, killing loneliness. There was
nothing repulsive about him, I was only sorry that I
could not fulfill his wish. When I refused him there

remained no tenseness between us, our understanding
for one another had at this moment been only increased.
For a long time we lay and talked to each other until I
sank into half sleep, and it was then that I heard my
name being called, a long drawn-out, icy cry, that cut
through the noise of the freight yards, where wheels
were rolling on frozen rails, brakes squealing, where the
crashings of car couplings being engaged were being
propagated from car to car, it penetrated me, a cry in my
mother's voice. And my parents became resigned when
they got the letter from the Authority, they gave up on
me, but nevertheless, with his sense of the practical, my
father tried to make it an orderly leave-taking, and I
was sent money, given a trial year, by the end of which
I was to show I was equal to a painter's calling. Now I
was on my own, all to myself, no one to keep an eye on
me, no one to fence me in, I could make of my day what
I pleased, and so undertake the impossible, to be done
with my old self and create an existence of my own.
There I stood in the city of Prague and had to prove myself, and I looked for a room in this city, a room that
would take me in, in which I could find myself, I walked
about in the strange city and the streets were hung with
black flags and muted drums were beaten and a coffin
was borne to the grave on a mount through the ranks of
the silent crowds. There I stand before alien doors, speak
brokenly in a foreign tongue, ask for a room, am led
by strangers down corridors where the air is stale and
stuffy. I intrude upon these strangers, force my way into
their apartments, I have never seen these people before,

and they know nothing about me and I expect them to give me a room. These fat women, these lean women, these poorly dressed widows, these dolled-up *demimondaines,* they open the doors of the rooms and switch the light on and the light is always feeble so that one does not notice how worn-out the room is, and I stand before a dimness of furniture, gloomy shapes which try to look like chairs, tables, wardrobes, beds, enveloped in a smokiness of nightmare wallpaper, and always, somewhere, the big nail sticks out of the wall, the nail on which to hang oneself. Until I finally find a room with its own entrance, a studio, dilapidated, dusty, with sooted windows, the ruins of a bedstead, with boxes and planks from which a table and a seat could be constructed. This room appeals to me, it is sick, it is spotted and burst open with sores, it shows me my wretchedness, it shows me the lowness of my estate. So I settled down in the foreign city, I found a lair into which other strangers had crept before me, and which would serve someone else as a flop. In this brief interval I made it livable for myself in my stony den in the middle of a great pile of stone, and surrounded myself with scrawls, hieroglyphs intended to give notice that I lived here, surrounded myself with magic signs, spells, with which I wanted to frighten away the evil spirits of loneliness. I lived for a whole year in this city. The city, with its ranks of streets, its architectures piled one atop the other, its gateways, bridges, and golden statues of my life, and in this framework the long walks and conversations with Max took place, along the banks of the river or on the slopes of the

vineyards, in the parks, and in the outer framework lay
the great Academy building among trees in which the
birds chirped, in this external frame the hours of work
passed away in the communal studio, with my fellow
students in front of the model or the still life, scraping
the brush on the canvas, in the smell of oil paints and
turpentine. The inner levels of my existence, however,
were enclosed by the room, this dwelling-place in which
I could hide. Relieved of my parents and my teachers, I
took over the tyranny over myself. Nobody could have
been harder and more ruthless than I was to myself. At
daybreak I forced myself out of bed and began my work.
The lessons at the academy were merely a formal justifi-
cation for my stay in this city, my actual achievements
were like blood oozing out after torture. I punched myself in the ribs, I spat on my hands and slapped my face
with them, I punished my tiredness and inattention by
depriving myself of food and with all this drudgery it
did finally come about that pictures rose up in me and
slowly, tentatively were projected onto the panels before
me. Memories of the surroundings of my earliest childhood re-echoed in these pictures, interspersed with the
impressions and reflections of later years, I tried to recognize myself in these pictures, I tried to heal myself
with these pictures, and they were full of the leaden
heaviness of my isolation and the explosive glow of my
pent-up despair. The evocation of these visions brought
me no release, the visions came to me as to a drowning
man, and the bodily experiments I carried on beside my
intellectual exertions led me to the brink of madness. In

the past years I had several times tried and failed to have
sexual intercourse with a woman. A few days before my
departure for England I tested myself with a prostitute. I
was still dressed in mourning after Margit's funeral. I
thought now I must prove myself, now I must begin my
new life as a man. The woman took off her skirt and
placed herself with legs astraddle over a pail and pissed
into the pail. I did not even try to undress. I gave her the
money and departed. In London I came across a woman
who invited me into her apartment. First of all she sent
me to have a bath, for I was dirty and had wandered
around town for some days in an attempt to break away.
She came to me in black, transparent silk. She tried hard
to get me going but she had two little Pekinese dogs lying on the bed who distracted me with their squeaking
and sniffing and their licking tongues. She did not want
any money from me, she wanted me as her lover, perhaps wanted to pay my way, too, but it did not appeal to
me. I ascribed this failure to my outward lack of freedom, nevertheless sensed it had deeper roots. Even now,
when there was no one to stop me from bringing a
woman up to my room, and no one to disturb us, a pro-
hibition, a curse, paralyzed me. Outside in the world
beyond there had been kisses and close embraces, I had
been gripped by physical desires, but now in the con-
tainment of my own room, when the naked, bodily acts
were imminent, I felt only coldness and futility. I explored the warm, strange skin, the limbs and joints, the
soft parts of the flesh. With the flat of my hand and my
eyes I had carnal knowledge of the curves of shoulders,

breasts, hips, belly, thighs, and my conscious mind pieced these perceptions together into a concept of woman, but my function as a man was not awakened thereby, I found myself faced with an insoluble task. The woman's movements indicating sexual excitement scared me, I knew that her sexual parts, now heaving up and down, were waiting for me, but I lacked the key to set the mechanism of this union in motion. I tried to find something in the woman's face that could help me to overcome the chasm of strangeness. Her eyes were shut, her half-open mouth breathed heavily. Behind the closed eyes lay the world of another human being, who wanted my most intimate closeness. When her eyes opened and I caught her longing look, I could feel for a second's duration the possibility of entering her, but straight-away the meaning of our being together was lost again in intangibles. My fingers stroked her pubic hair and the lips of her vagina, which opened up between her yielding outspread thighs, I saw the rosy and brownish inside of the wet lips, I imagined the depths that wanted to take me in, yet I felt no enticement, felt only the impossibility of it all. Suddenly I could see Margit's body in front of me, as she had once offered herself to me, and I saw the bones of this body far from me in a hole in the earth and I sprang up and only wanted to be alone and the stranger who had followed me into my lair threw on her clothes and fled in terror. She, who was dead, I could love, I could give myself to her, I need no longer have any fear of her, she asked nothing from me. To her who was dead, I could escape and no one could find out if my love was genuine. Whenever I failed in my attempts with the living, the living woman in my presence, I consoled myself with the dead, the childlike woman of the past. From a living woman I could not hide, in her presence I had to come out of my confinedness, reach out far into an outer world. And that meant being swallowed up, surrendering myself. As a child I had once seen my mother's genitals, she was standing bent over in her nightdress and between her heavy thighs gaped the dark, hair-fringed hole. As then, when I had stared in vertiginous alarm into my mother's great crack, so now my gaze was riveted on the genitals of a living woman of the present, my fingers opened the wet, soft lips, under whose swellings and recesses was concealed the secret of all existence, and if I could penetrate into this sucking depth I would penetrate to the very core of life. In my impotence I looked for women who wanted to be hurt and who put up with the endless preliminaries that always had no result. These women had no names, their faces were blurred, they were merely an *idée fixe* for me, I drew them into my madness, I felt them out and searched them out, and sometimes for a few moments they were like my dead sister, and their faces were surrounded by wire frames and the head was fastened to the neck with screws and tubes and I worked feverishly in this technical confusion to restore the control mechanism that could bring her back to life again and sometimes the mouth moved and sometimes the eyelids twitched and I whispered, Wake up, wake up, and around me in the half-dark room the surfaces of

pictures and the boxes and plants and frames stood out
and the easel rose up like a gallows, and white papers
shone out of the shadows, and then I pulled the naked
body from the bed onto the floor and we wallowed in
the soot and crawled around between the planks and
pots and embraced each other in contorted positions. I
could not talk to anyone about it, not even to Max. Once
I went to a doctor who in a newspaper ad promised to
cure impotence. He sold me a powder that I was to take
mixed with soda water. There was no other remedy.
There was only hang on or kick the bucket. If I do not
kick the bucket, perhaps sometime I will find a woman
whose look and gestures, whose voice and caresses, will
suddenly break through the layer of ice. And one day I
will find out what this opening underneath her body is
like, this entrance to life, and I will thrust myself into the
silky warmth, I will let myself be sucked round by life's
wet, soft mouth, I will burrow into it, and unload a part
of my life into the greedy, viviparous deep. My mouth,
too, will trace out the opened, mussel-colored lips, my
tongue will lap up the sweet taste to the tenderly haired
vagina, incredible that I should have recoiled from it
before. And then perhaps one day I will discover that
there is no loneliness, that this whole culture of loneliness was only a misunderstanding, only a convention, a
lack of fantasy, an impoverishment of feeling, for how
can there be loneliness if one can come so close to someone else, so deeply pervade each other. And this possibility must have existed then too, otherwise if it had
not been there I should have thrown myself out of the

window. Max told me once how in the World War and in the Spanish Civil War he had heard dying men calling out to their mothers, Mamma, Mamma, they had shouted. There lay these finished men, perhaps fallen for something they believed in, and the last thing they screamed for was the abyss from which they once had crawled. One cannot live unless one loves this great crack. Oh life, oh great cunt of life. In the moment of death we scream for you. Such realizations came with lightning rapidity and immediately afterward I could no longer conceive them. But they left their mark behind. They occur again. I shout, Yes, that is how it is, and I no longer know what I meant. Oh cunt of life. Now I can throw my arms around my mother again, can weep on her riddled body, can cover her sunken mouth, her decrepit cheeks with kisses, can stroke her worn hands, can now press close, close to her naked body, to her sucked-out breasts, to her scarred belly, press between her vein-swollen thighs, close, close to the hole whence I came. In Prague, in this first place where I wanted to find my way to freedom, I found only darkness and self-destruction. When my appointed time was at an end after this year, the pressure of the outside world had fiendishly grown. In a preliminary practice for later disaster the sirens had wailed and in the blacked-out city invisible crowds pressed into the streets with clattering footsteps and murmuring voices. Here and there shone the dancing glow of a cigarette, and suppressed shouts and whistles rose up out of the ebbing and flowing throng. The inhabitants of the city were like one single widely branching black body, wholly given over to one single uncertain expectancy. When the siren sounded again we stood still, as if beneath the rushing wings of some mythological monster. We stood in darkness in the foreboding of an apocalyptic time. When the lights in all the streets flamed on again all at once, we greeted them with a thousandfold cry of hope in life renewed, yet for a long time we had been conscious of lawlessness and disintegration lurking in the streets. And on one of the last days I stood with Peter Kien, a friend from the Academy, in a bright street and we held between us a large picture I had painted, a picture that showed a burning city, and Peter Kien stared up into the air and drew in his breath with a sobbing sound, and I saw a dark mass of rags come falling down from above, and as the rags smacked onto the stony pavement of the street I saw what sort of rags they were. The dark pile of rags had a head, and blood streamed from the head, and the rags were a body that huddled itself together, that waltzed over on its side, pressed knees hard into its belly, and then lay still, stiffened, like an embryo in a great pregnant mother made of stone. People came running from all sides and we held up the burning city to them. Peter Kien's breath came in sobs. Flee, Peter Kien, don't stay here. Flee, hide yourself, you with your hopelessly open face, with your disconcerted staring gaze behind the thick prisms of your glasses, flee before it is too late. But Peter Kien remained behind. Peter Kien was murdered and burned. I escaped. I sent my pictures to my parents, packed my knapsack and wandered south, I

found a village by a mountain lake, then I went up to the
north where my parents had escaped with their possessions. When I was tramping along the road to the south,
it seemed continually as if the dark rag was falling from
a great height and I saw above me the open window,
high up in a house in the stone city, and I imagined the
room through which a living man had just run, I saw
the window from inside the room, the blue pool of
the window, I experienced the irrevocable decision, the
overcoming of the last resistance. Alone with my own
footsteps on the smooth ribbon of country road, I
rushed through the room, this last room of a life, a red
carpet with a Persian design lay on the floor of the room,
and in front of the sofa stood an oval table with carved
bowlegs, and on the table stood a violet crystal vase, and
on the wall hung a mirror with an ornate gold frame and
the window could be seen in the mirror, and my rush to
the window. I imagined the second in which everything
solid vanished, the second in which I rushed up to the
window sill and hurled myself out into the blue waters
of emptiness. In the very first instant after crossing the
frontier from which return was no longer possible, I
flew as in a dream, it was as if I could fly upward, light as
a bird, I would mount and mount, with outspread arms,
how had I summoned up the energy for this leap,
whence had I taken the courage for this leap, in the very
first instant after the second of the explosion I flew on
without gravity in an ecstasy; the air rippled around me,
I breathed no more, I was enraptured, my eyes were
closed. It was Death that had seized me, it was the power

of Death that had taken hold of me in the room and
hurled me out of the window, the leap was inconceivable
if Death had not become voluptuousness, then a current
enveloped me that sucked me downward, suddenly I got
no further, the heaviness of the whole world hung upon
me, and ever stronger and stronger was the force of the
current that sucked me into the depths. Landscapes re-
volved past me, I heard the beat of my footsteps and felt
the falling and the terror at suddenly realizing that it
was too late, and then I lay smashed and shattered in the
city's stony womb, I rested at the roadside, drank water
from brooks and wells, stayed overnight at hostels, and
after weeks reached the lake, ran through thickets and
down pebbly slopes to the shore, threw off knapsack
and clothes, and plunged into the tepid water. I lay on
my back, moving my hands and feet only slightly, and
around about rose the mountains in the haze of twilight.
White villages shimmered out of the violet-green shadows and everywhere bright bells were ringing. It was as
if I were floating backward, I hovered in the depths of a
vast chalice, whose rim dissolved in the gold dust of the
sunken sun. All heaviness and oppressiveness passed
away, washed off by the light embraces of the water, ab-
sorbed and evaporated in the mother-of-pearl light.
Here by this lake I found an intermediate kingdom, here
arose the beginnings of another relaxed, almost happy
existence. It was an existence that hung from a single
thin thread, but curiously enough I found in this outwardly ever more uncertain state of things a tinge of
inner harmony. Previously I had felt no contact with the

countryside, rather I had felt lost in it, an outcast and
abandoned to transience, and only in towns could I feel
as if I belonged, but there in this mountain scenery,
these vineyards, deciduous woods and ancient villages
pieced together out of rough stones, here in the mild-
ness of early summer, which would soon become a
shimmering tropical warmth, I experienced hours of
vegetative peace. I lost the manic need to be active, and
could lie on the shores of the lake in the sun or in the
dry grass of a clearing in the wood without being trou-
bled by a bad conscience. And when I wanted to draw or
write something, I could wait for a long time and medi-
tate beforehand, and drawing and writing were not so
important, I could also leave them be, it was more important that I existed, that I was alive, and before working I had first to learn how to experience. I strolled
through the thick, dark green woods, and even though
at times, faced by this luxuriant growth and the fragrance of rotting vegetation, a sudden fear rose up in
me, this was outweighed by a desire to explore, a *joie de
vivre* under whose influence I often found myself sing-
ing and laughing in utter solitude. And here in a warm,
starlit night for the first time I got into a woman's body,
we stood embracing on a balcony overlooking the lake,
and she drew me into her room, onto her bed, and there
was no struggle and no strain, it was effortlessly easy, life
played with us and I no longer rebelled against it. Early
the following morning I stood below in the courtyard, I
washed my face and my hands in the trickling water and
on my genitals I still felt the warmth of the inside of the

female body, and in the village a cock crowed and animals were stirring in their stalls, and I straightened and
stretched myself in a new self-awareness. But after the
elation came the depression. It was not the daily increas-
ing pressure of the outside world that led to the extin-
guishing of these days, the break took place within me, I
could not endure in such brightness. Incapable of living
on my own energy, I had to return to my parents' home.
My father had transferred his factory with the machines
and capital to the new country and the accustomed
home had grown up again under my mother's hands in
the interior of the new house. I came back as the Prodigal Son, to whom was offered the grace of a place to stay.
A folder with drawings, a couple of notebooks with
notes were my sole possessions. My pictures, which I
had entrusted to my mother, were no longer there.
When she was preparing to move, she had carried my
pictures into the cellar, chopped them up with an axe,
and burned them in the furnace. She explained this destruction as a safety precaution. She had feared that my
gloomy, weird pictures would arouse the suspicions of
the frontier authorities. She had saved the home. The
pictures, an expression of disease, had had to be sacri-
ficed. I returned to this home and I had been robbed of
the only signs of my strength. With her own hands she
had destroyed the picture world of my youth, the dances
of death, the apocalyptic visions, and the dream landscapes. With this destruction she had freed herself from
the threat that these pictures had exerted on the orderliness and protectedness of her home. I stood there
empty-handed like a tramp. I had no other choice but to

enter my father's factory. The factory was still encased in scaffolding. Next door in a small green shack the temporary office and warehouse had been set up. Here stood the machine parts and precision instruments, packed in wood shavings and corrugated paper, here stood barrels and cans full of paints and chemicals, and in the piled-up boxes lay the materials that would later be colored and printed in the factory. The cement mixer rumbled the whole day outside in the courtyard, and inside in the hut everything rattled and trembled with it. I sat at my typewriter and hacked down the almost incomprehensible words that my father had dictated. Although I had to invent half of the business letters, everything developed according to plan. Answers came with the mail and were acknowledged, the building of the factory progressed, through the cracked windowpane I could see the walls growing. Agents and future clients appeared, collections of patterns were worked out, contracts signed, while the door was being wrenched open and shut with a crash, while laborers, skilled workers and engineers came in, spread out and discussed construction blueprints, while dust rose in whirls and the naked bulb on the ceiling, fed by the factory's own generator, shook, flickered and from time to time went out. It was a dark time of year with much rain and mist, and it was hoped to have the building finished before the winter. And everything went according to plan. We lived here in the Wild West, but a few yards away from us machines were mounted onto their bases, cables, steam, and water systems were laid, a few yards away from us a huge, functional composition in glass and concrete arose, wrapped up in a network of wires and rods. With the first snow we shifted into a new world that smelled of paint and polish and that still resounded to the sound of hammers and saws. The workmen and clerks were inspected and introduced to their new activities by a handful of specialists. In the dyeworks, in the scouring mill, in the finishing rooms and in the printing rooms, in the laboratories, in the room where the colors were mixed, in the pattern room, in the warehouse and in the office everything was set in motion, at first slowly and fumblingly, but full of confidence and enthusiasm. This was my new music, the song of the machines, and statistics and schedules were my poems, I was a workman among workmen, but I was not one of them, I was the owner's son. But I had nothing to do with the owner, so I remained a foreign body among the large throbbing machinery that steadily grew into its melody. I lived in a vacuum between the world of my parents and the world of the workmen. If I had been anonymous and unanchored to my home, I could perhaps have struck up a friendship, a communion in physical work, with a girl perhaps, one of the weavers or a female warehouse clerk, a simple bodily relationship, but that too is a dream, in this dream I deny myself, in this dream I deny that there is only one thing for me, the struggle for the independence of my work. So long as I suppressed this struggle, everything else was bound to be bleak for me, I comprehended nothing of the living conditions of the workers, of their struggle, their problems, for the most elementary thing was not granted me, the chance to carry out my own work. But who here carried out his own work.

Sometimes I looked into the organization of this structure in which each of them was cocooned in his movements, but in which no one inwardly participated, I saw
these absent-minded faces, these mechanical activities,
and the extraordinary lostness and extinction of the
lunch hours, people played cards, solved crossword
puzzles, and such personality as there was in them dissolved into a shapeless pulp. Here one found a livelihood, one could earn what one needed for the rent,
food, and a few pleasures, and perhaps there was nothing more, perhaps this was all, no one seemed to ask for
more or at most only a better flat, richer food, and new
means of amusement. In this existence, with no chance
of starting discussions about problems of self-expression
and formation where one could feel concerned about
more vital matters, all my personal projects fell victim to
the doubt that they no longer had any *raison d'être*, and
that it was only diseased selfishness on my part that had
ever led me to concern myself with them. Perhaps I
lived in this factory as all the others lived, in the mornings I came in with the stream of workmen and carried
out my appointed tasks and in the evenings I left again,
in the stream of the others, and a dull dissatisfaction and
vague dreams filled me, just as all the others were filled
with them. By day there was only work, nothing but being harnessed to the production process, by day only
this unique, important business of manufacturing fab-
rics for curtains and clothing, and sometimes this
uniqueness and importance took on feverish proportions, as I saw it then, whereupon I experienced in depth
the way things were made, how the raw material was

swallowed up in the factory's maw and, amid the pound-
ing of powerful machines, proceeded through the stages
of its metamorphosis, rolled through vats and drums in
which it was prepared, steamed and drained in the wash
room, came alive in the dye house where the dye boss's
control booth hung like a glass ship in the steamy mist,
and was slung forth by rotating metal arms, to be sucked
up by rollers with broad metal lips, and then fluttered in
long ribbons onto the rubber-covered tables of the
printing rooms, where in the tropical heat half-naked
workers bent over it and let it drink in the colors of the
printed patterns, and now one could already guess their
future existence, heavy and gleaming with flowers and
butterflies and figurines the materials hung stretched
out to dry in the long rooms behind whose windows the
sky reflected their colors, then they were snatched into a
new vat, dragged through new streams, and made com-
pliant by a hail of blows from little hammers, and then
they rolled light and fragrant off the belts and were di-
vided up and wrapped up in rolls and supplied with labels, and many of them bore the names of goddesses
and their earthly existences began and they shone in the
streets and woods as dresses, they fluttered as curtains
from windows, and finally they lay faded and torn on
the rubbish heaps at the edge of cities. And we kept on
producing them. Ceaselessly we kept on, while outside a
world fell into pieces. The war did not open my eyes.
The frustrated struggle for my vocation had put me in a
state of derangement. My defeat was not the defeat of
the emigrant in face of the difficulties of living in exile,

but the defeat of one who does not dare to free himself
from his dependence. Emigrating had taught me nothing. Emigrating was for me a confirmation of the not-
belonging that I had experienced from my earliest
childhood. I had never possessed a native soil. I was left
untouched by the fact that the struggle that went on outside affected my existence also. I had never come to any
conclusions about the revolutionary conflicts in the
world. The effort I had made to find some means of expression for my existence had claimed all my awareness.
This period was for me a period of waiting, a period of
sleepwalking. I spent two years in the factory. I carried
out my work in the darkroom of the printing department, where by the feeble red glow of a safety light I
developed photos of sample designs, I carried out my
work in a little sealed room, deep in the bowels of the
roaring factory. Although his wish to see me employed
in his field had been granted, my father paid no more
attention to me. He never came to me with any questions. It was as if he sensed I would again desert him.
The hours I spent together with the family passed in the
same atmosphere of estrangement, I sat through one
part of the evening in my parents' company as if it were
a debt, silently turning the pages of a book or magazine,
while on the radio monotonous anonymous voices reported inconceivable events. Out of this period a cry
breaks out of me. Why have we squandered these days
and years, people living under the same roof, without
being able to speak to or hear each other. What sort of
disease is this that makes us so dreary, that fills us with

such distrust and reticence, that we can no longer look
one another in the eyes. And yet this period, which at
the time seemed completely dead to me, contained expressions of a secret life. At night in my room or on Sundays, pictures, drawings, poems, hidden expressions of
someone unknown and renounced came to life. In the
depth of this total isolation there was a quiet delibera-
tion as a result of which each month I put aside money
for the future. In the late summer of the second year the
break-up began with a violent blow. I had gone into the
woods to work. The buzzing of the mosquitoes was like
a light drone of bells; beetles and spiders rustled in the
dry foliage. I settled down at the side of a mountain lake.
I fell asleep, wishing that I might never wake again. I
dreamed of my way through this forest. There was the
old fear of being lost in the forest, of death in the bog,
among the ferns in utter stillness. On a narrow path I
encountered a man in a hunter's outfit, a hunting bag
and a gun over his shoulder. He went past me and it was
as if I had met him once before, a long time ago. Then
I wandered along a country road. The road led me
through an immeasurably wide and confused life. Again
I met the huntsman, he came straight toward me and I
had to step aside to let him pass. Hastily he raised his
hand in greeting. I came to a lake and let myself drift
into the water and out there in the brightness of blur-
ring reflections the huntsman popped up again in front
of me, I recognized him and awoke. On a holiday trip
many years before as a child I had met him in a wood.
There was the resinous tang of freshly felled fir trees,

and I twisted between my fingers a small round wooden disk that had fallen from the beginning of a bough of a sawed-off tree trunk. The huntsman appeared and asked me my name. I told him. He said, That's my name too. He asked me insistently where I lived. I told him the name of the town. He said, I live there too. He asked me what street. I named it and he said, I live on that street too. He asked me for the number of the house, I told him, and he said, So we live in the same house. He moved off and left me behind in unspeakable astonishment. With the warning of this dream in my mind I jumped up. I could not interpret the dream but only felt that a change had come about, that my life was governed by new forces. I saw my footsteps in the sand at the edge of the lake. For a moment the vision of these steps that had led me from my birth onward to this place filled me. In a single instant I saw the dark pattern of their track. I recognized it and forgot it again immediately and in fear at my past I ran up into the undergrowth. Birds fluttered out of the trees, the sky was blood-red from the sinking sun. And the uneasiness that had now begun could no longer be contained, after weeks and months of slow inner changes, after relapses into weakness and discouragement, I took leave of my parents. The wheels of the railway thumped away beneath me with their ceaseless hollow drumbeats and the forces of my flying forward screamed and sang in incantatory chorus. I was on my way to look for a life of my own.

THE NEVERSINK LIBRARY

THE NEVERSINK LIBRARY

THE NEVERSINK LIBRARY